EHEADS
LUCKY DAY

by Tedd Arnold
Martha Hamilton
and Mitch Weiss

illustrated by Tedd Arnold

HOLIDAY HOUSE · NEW YORK

For Will and Robin and Fizzy and Nanners
—T.A.

For Patti, who makes everyone
feel lucky to know her
—M.H. and M.W.

Text copyright © 2020 by Tedd Arnold, Martha Hamilton, and Mitch Weiss
Illustrations copyright © 2020 by Tedd Arnold
All Rights Reserved
HOLIDAY HOUSE is registered in the U.S. Patent and Trademark Office.
Printed and bound in April 2020 at Toppan Leefung, DongGuan City, China.
The artwork was rendered digitally using Photoshop software.
www.holidayhouse.com
First Edition
1 3 5 7 9 10 8 6 4 2

Library of Congress Cataloging-in-Publication Data

Names: Arnold, Tedd, author, illustrator. | Hamilton, Martha, author.
Weiss, Mitch, 1951- author.
Title: Noodleheads lucky day / by Tedd Arnold, Martha Hamilton, and Mitch
Weiss ; illustrated by Tedd Arnold.
Other titles: Lucky day
Description: First edition. | New York : Holiday House, [2020] | Series:
[Noodleheads ; 5] | Audience: Ages 6-9. | Audience: Grades 2-3.
Summary: "Brothers Mac and Mac are SO lucky that everything goes well -
even when their frenemy Meatball plays tricks on them"— Provided by publisher.
Identifiers: LCCN 2019055014 | ISBN 9780823440023 (hardback)
Subjects: LCSH: Graphic novels. | CYAC: Graphic novels. | Fools and
jesters—Fiction. | Luck—Fiction. | Brothers—Fiction. | Humorous stories.
Classification: LCC PZ7.7.A757 Nos 2020 | DDC 741.5/973—dc23
LC record available at https://lccn.loc.gov/2019055014

ISBN: 978-0-8234-4002-3 (hardcover)

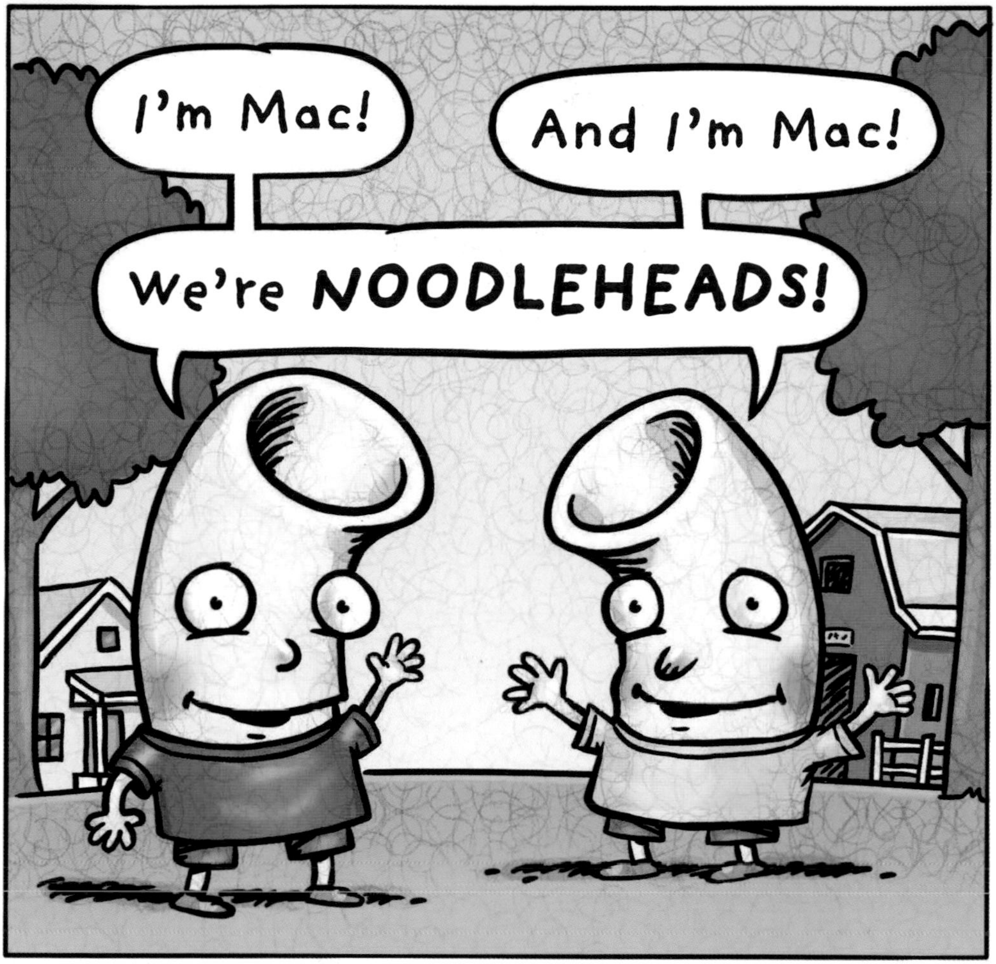
I'm Mac!
And I'm Mac!
We're **NOODLEHEADS!**

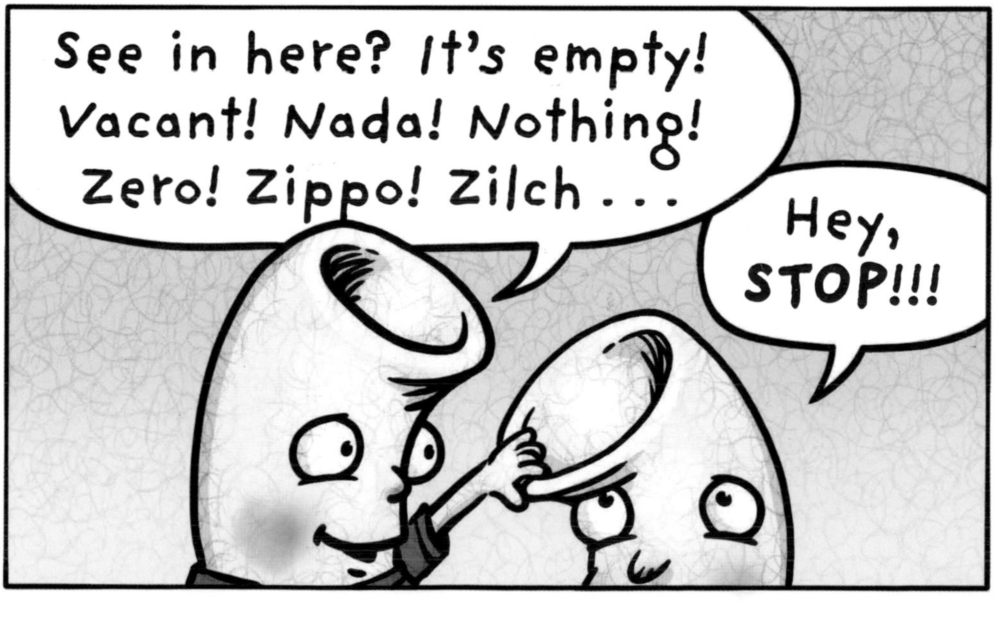
See in here? It's empty! Vacant! Nada! Nothing! Zero! Zippo! Zilch . . .
Hey, **STOP!!!**

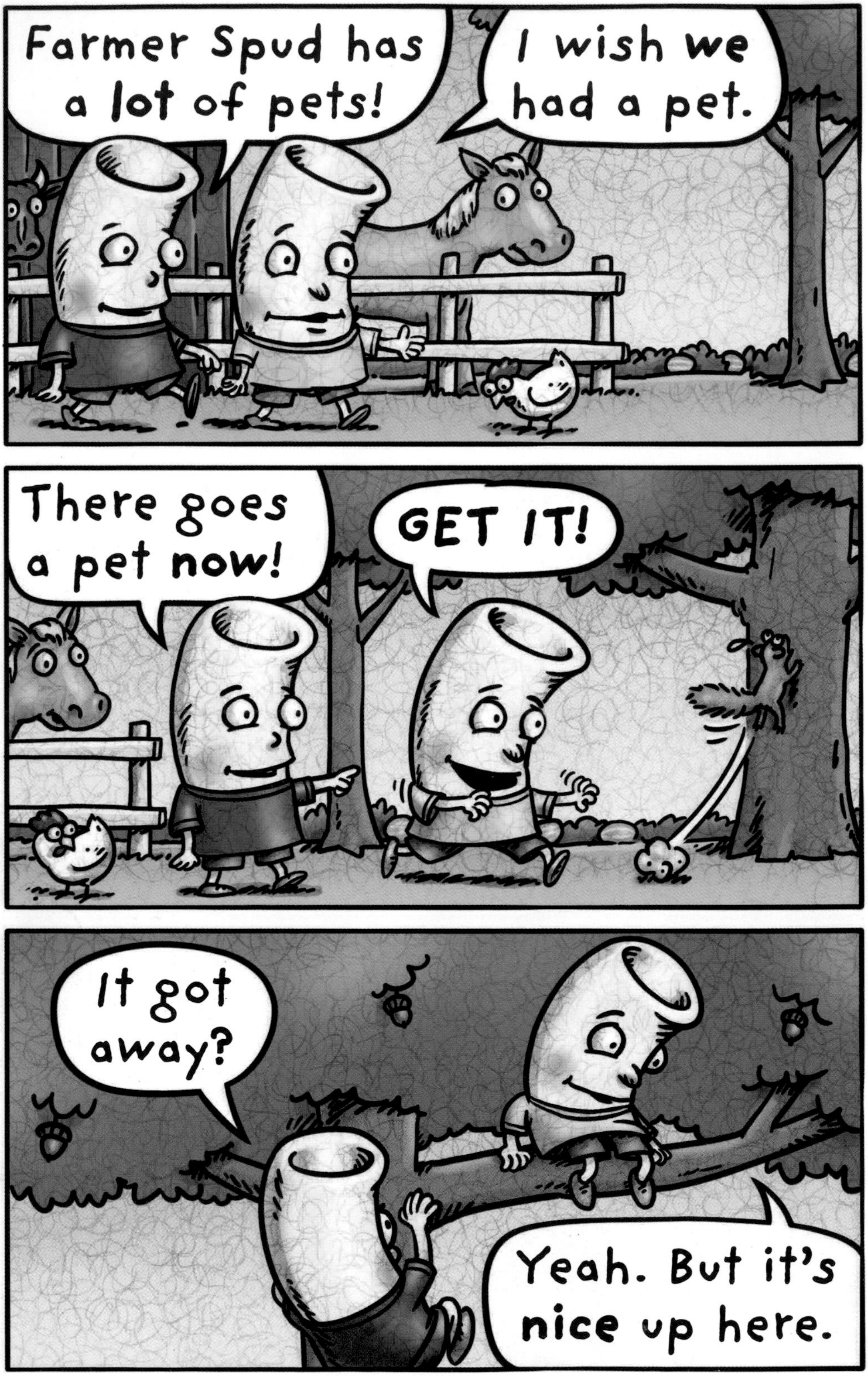
Farmer Spud has a lot of pets!
I wish we had a pet.
There goes a pet now!
GET IT!
It got away?
Yeah. But it's nice up here.

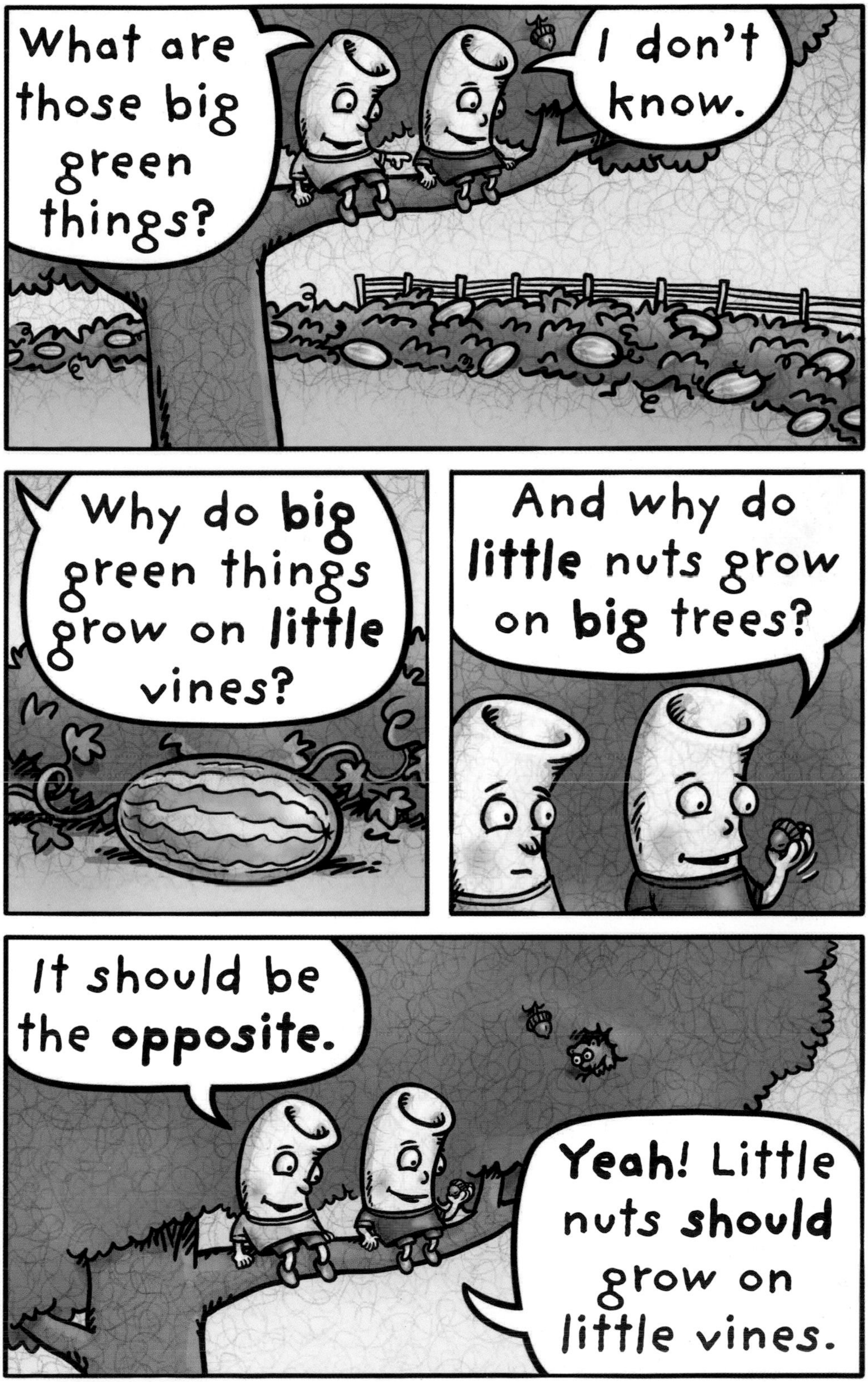
What are those big green things?
I don't know.
Why do **big** green things grow on **little** vines?
And why do **little** nuts grow on **big** trees?
It should be the **opposite.**
Yeah! Little nuts **should** grow on little vines.

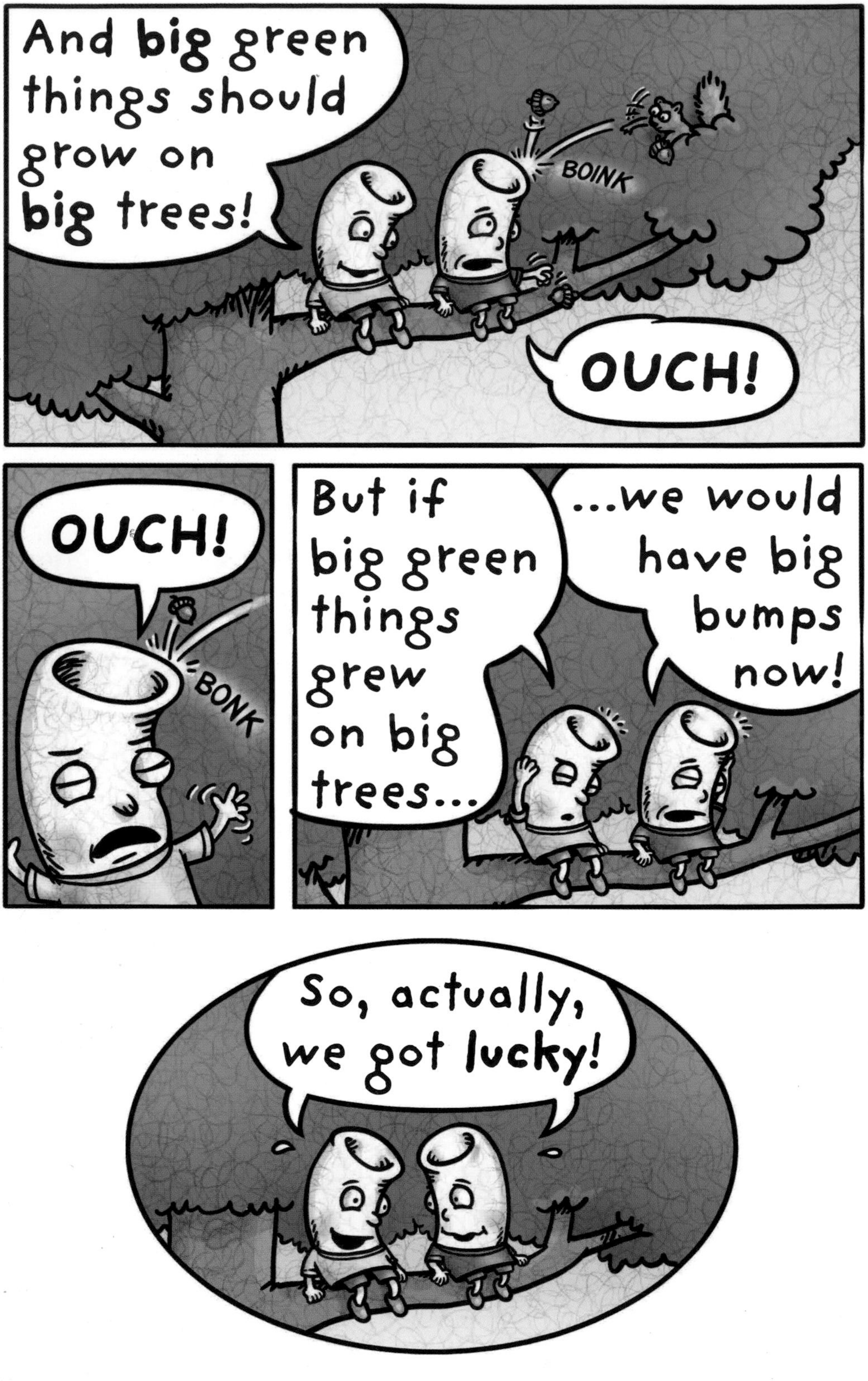
And big green things should grow on big trees!
BOINK
OUCH!
OUCH!
BONK
But if big green things grew on big trees...
...we would have big bumps now!
So, actually, we got lucky!

Noodleheads Lucky Day

Chapter 1

Looking for Trouble

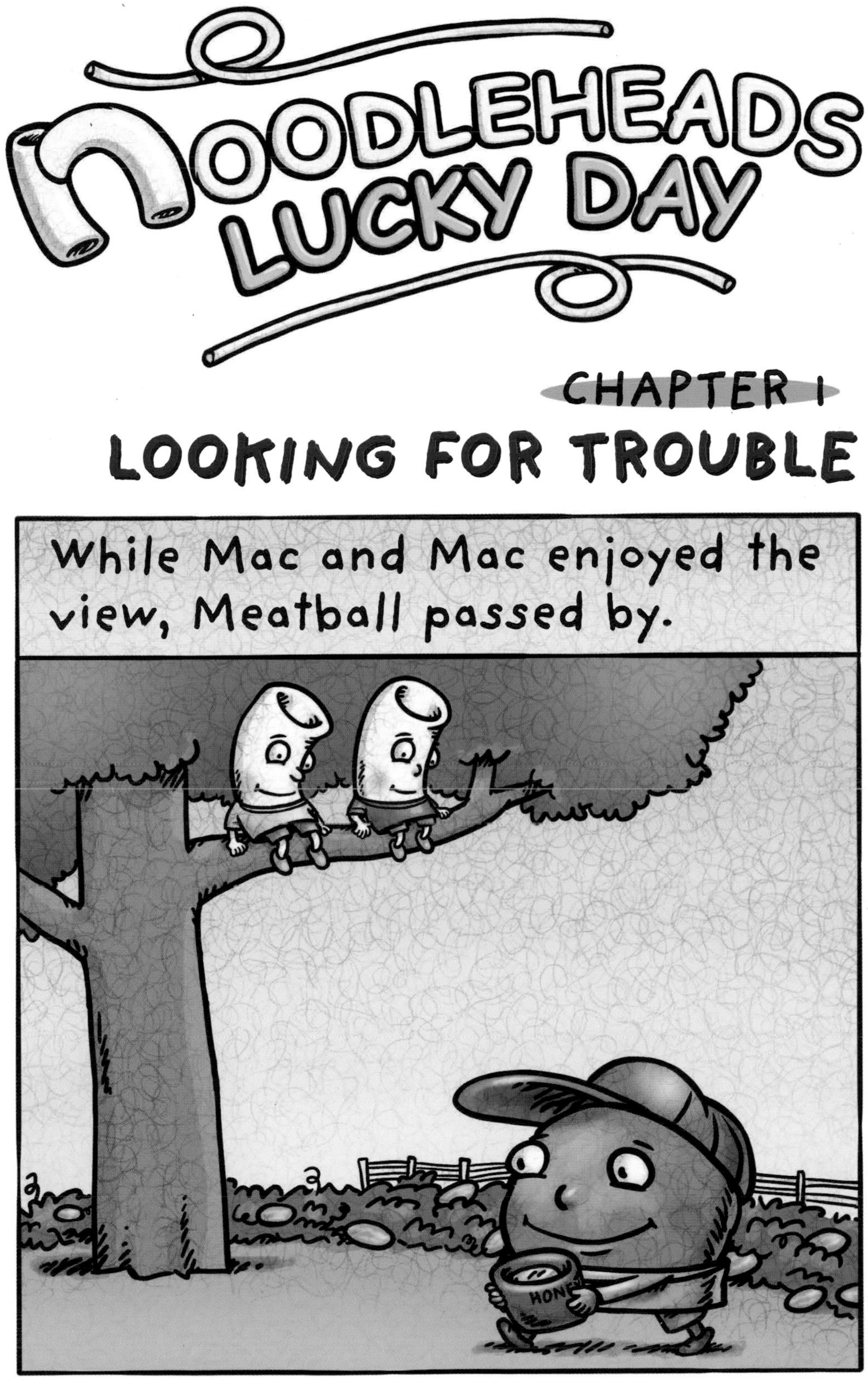
While Mac and Mac enjoyed the view, Meatball passed by.

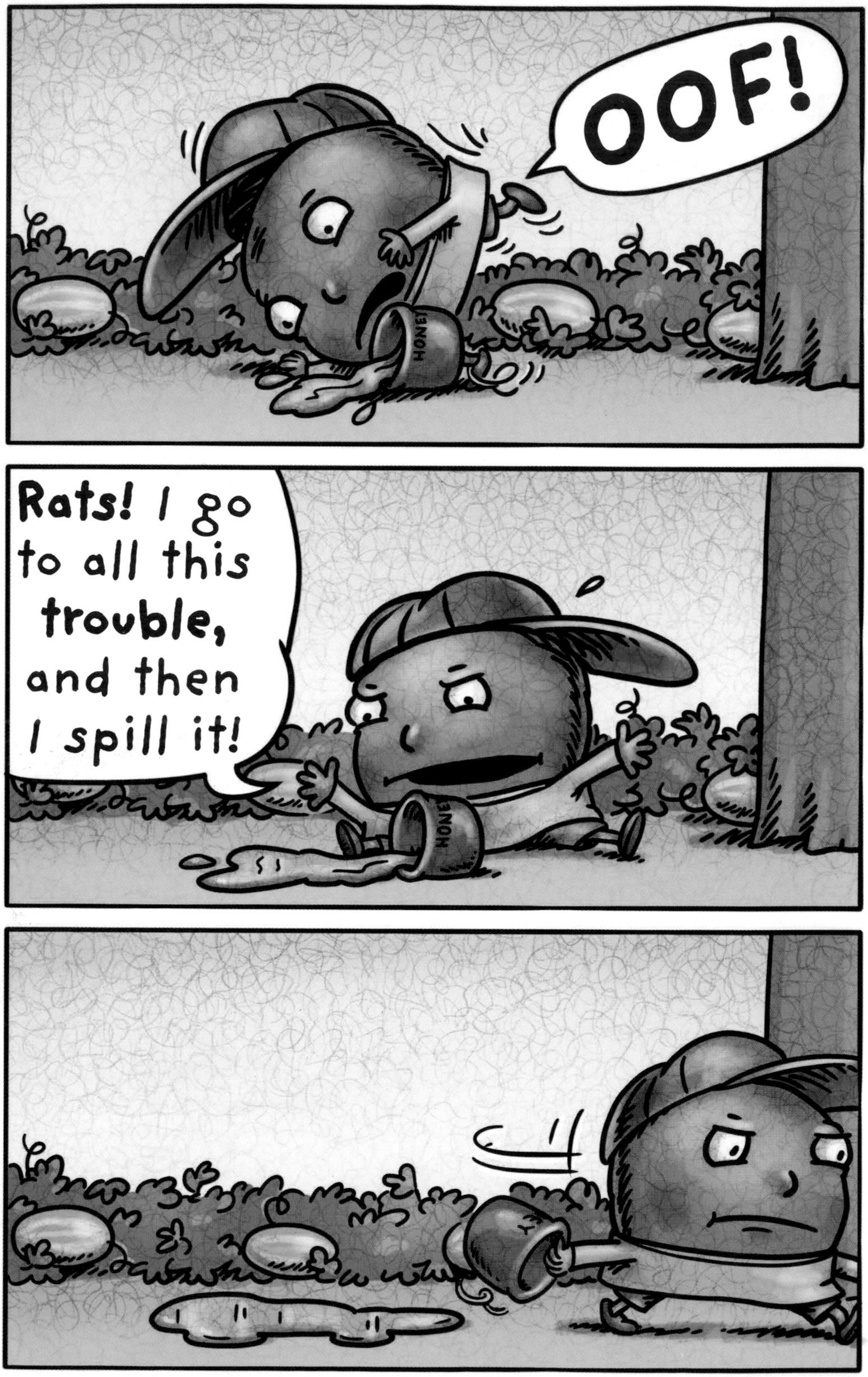
OOF!
HONEY
Rats! I go to all this trouble, and then I spill it!
HONEY

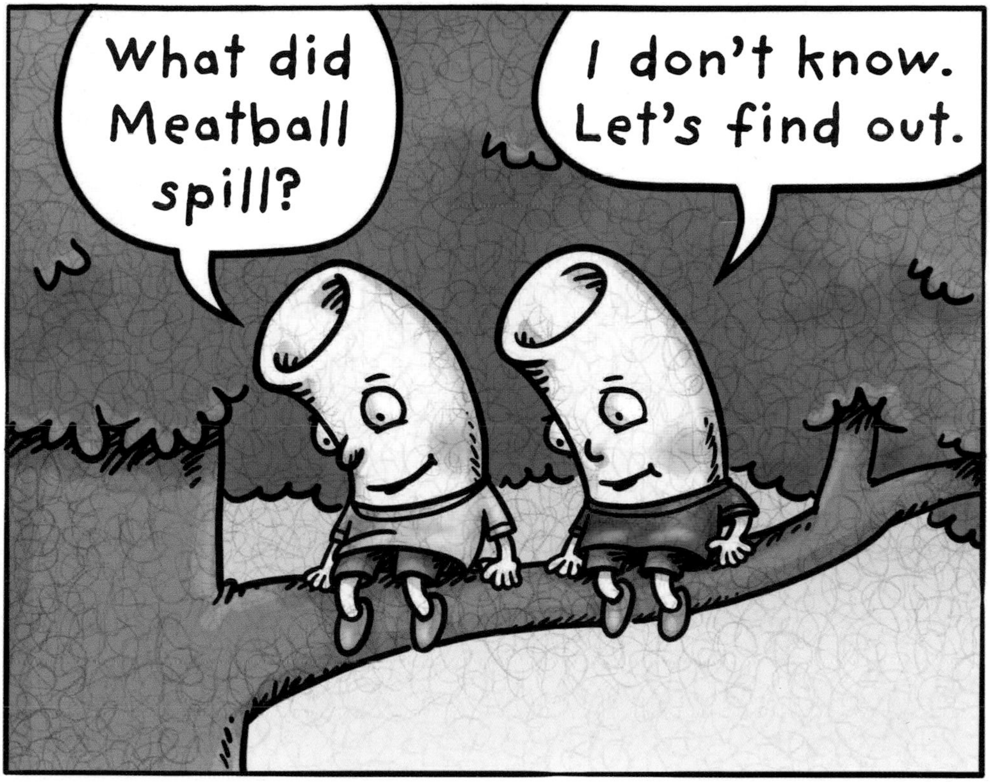
What did Meatball spill?
I don't know. Let's find out.

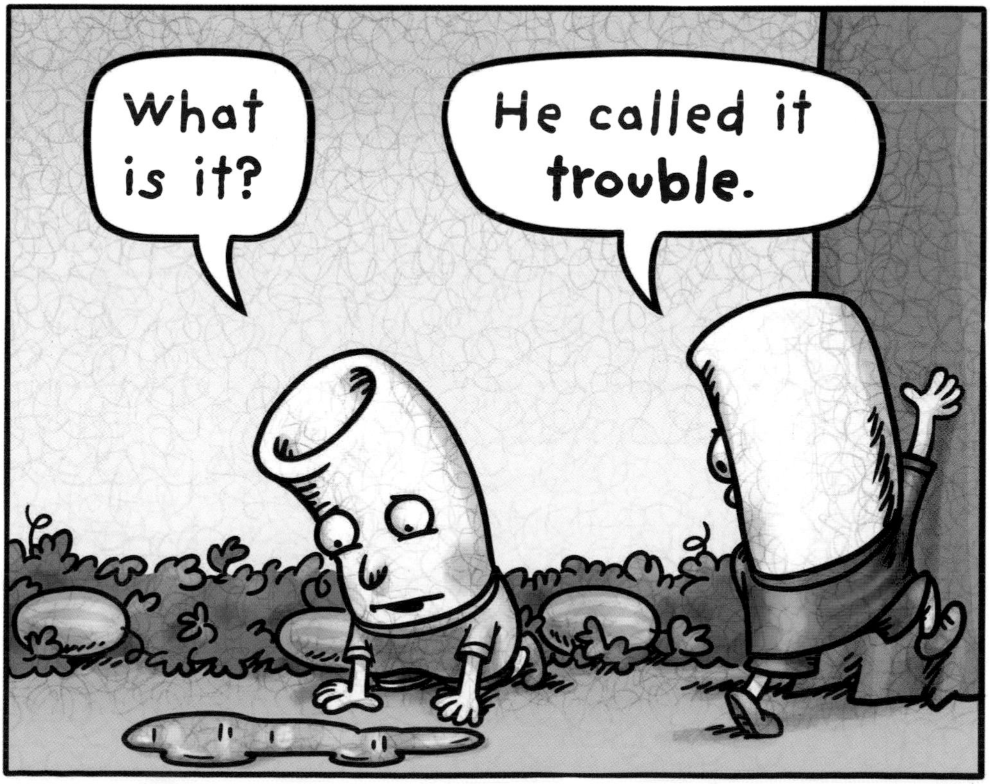
What is it?
He called it **trouble**.

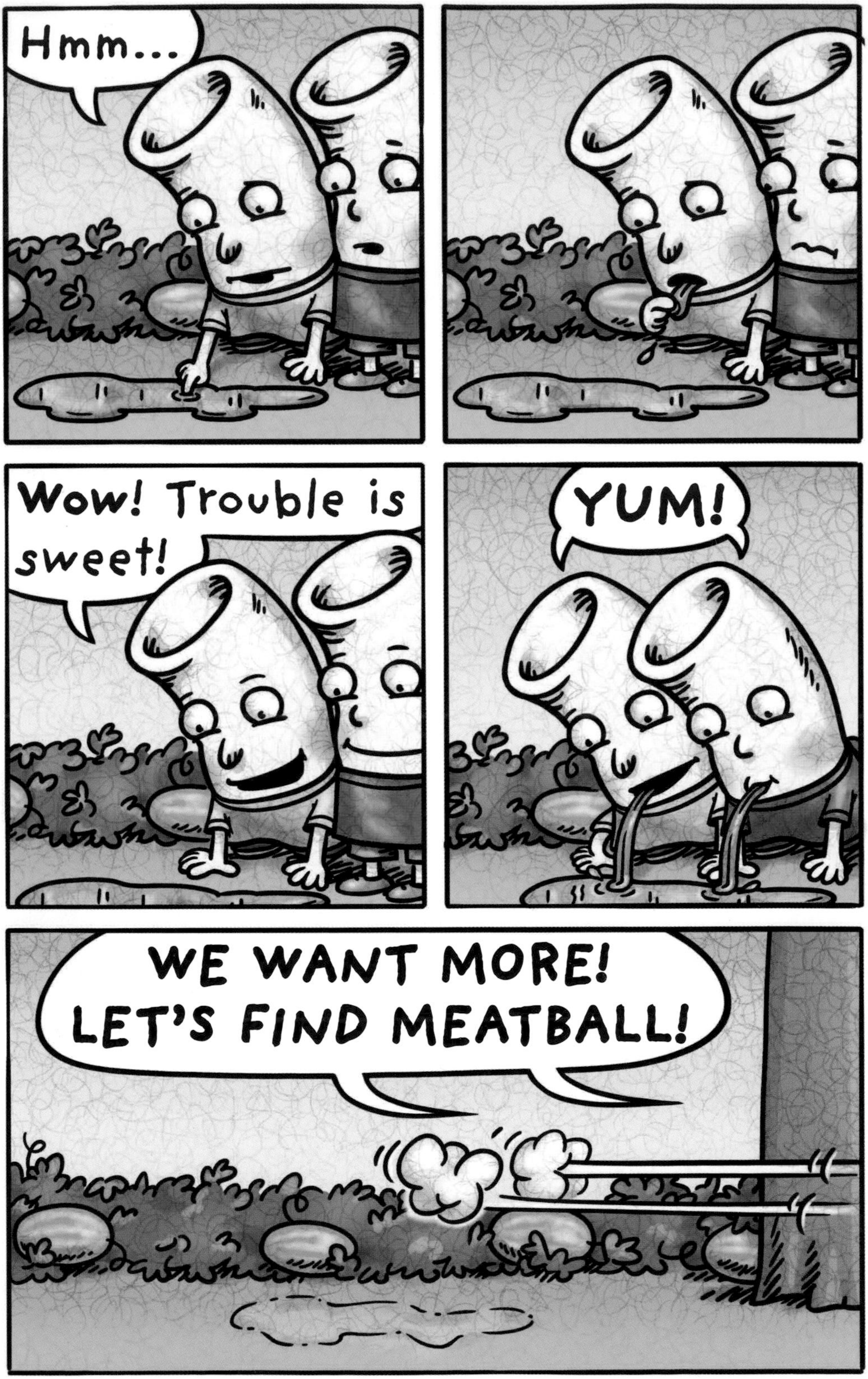
Hmm...
Wow! Trouble is sweet!
YUM!
WE WANT MORE! LET'S FIND MEATBALL!

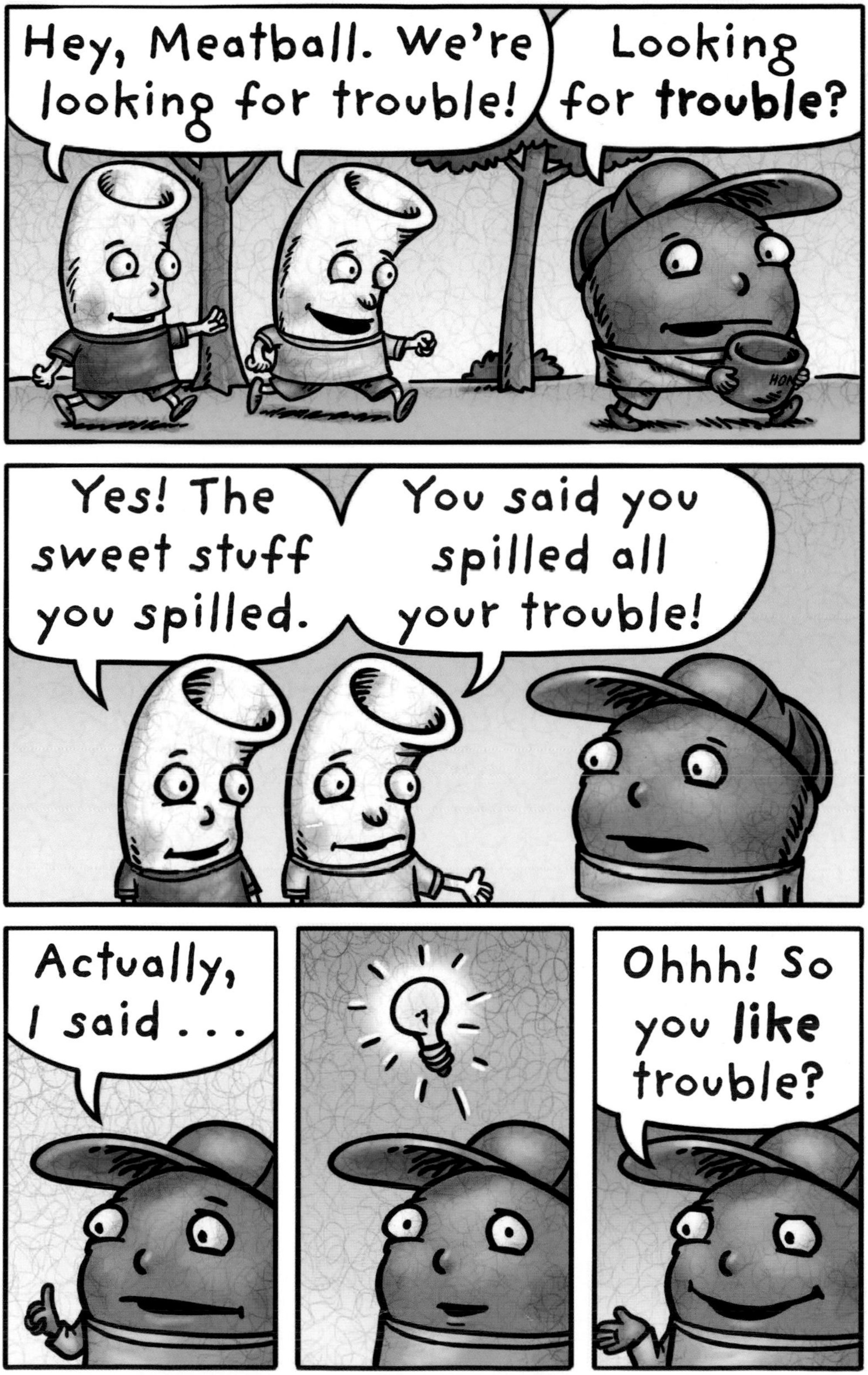
Hey, Meatball. We're looking for trouble!
Looking for trouble?
Yes! The sweet stuff you spilled.
You said you spilled all your trouble!
Actually, I said . . .
Ohhh! So you like trouble?

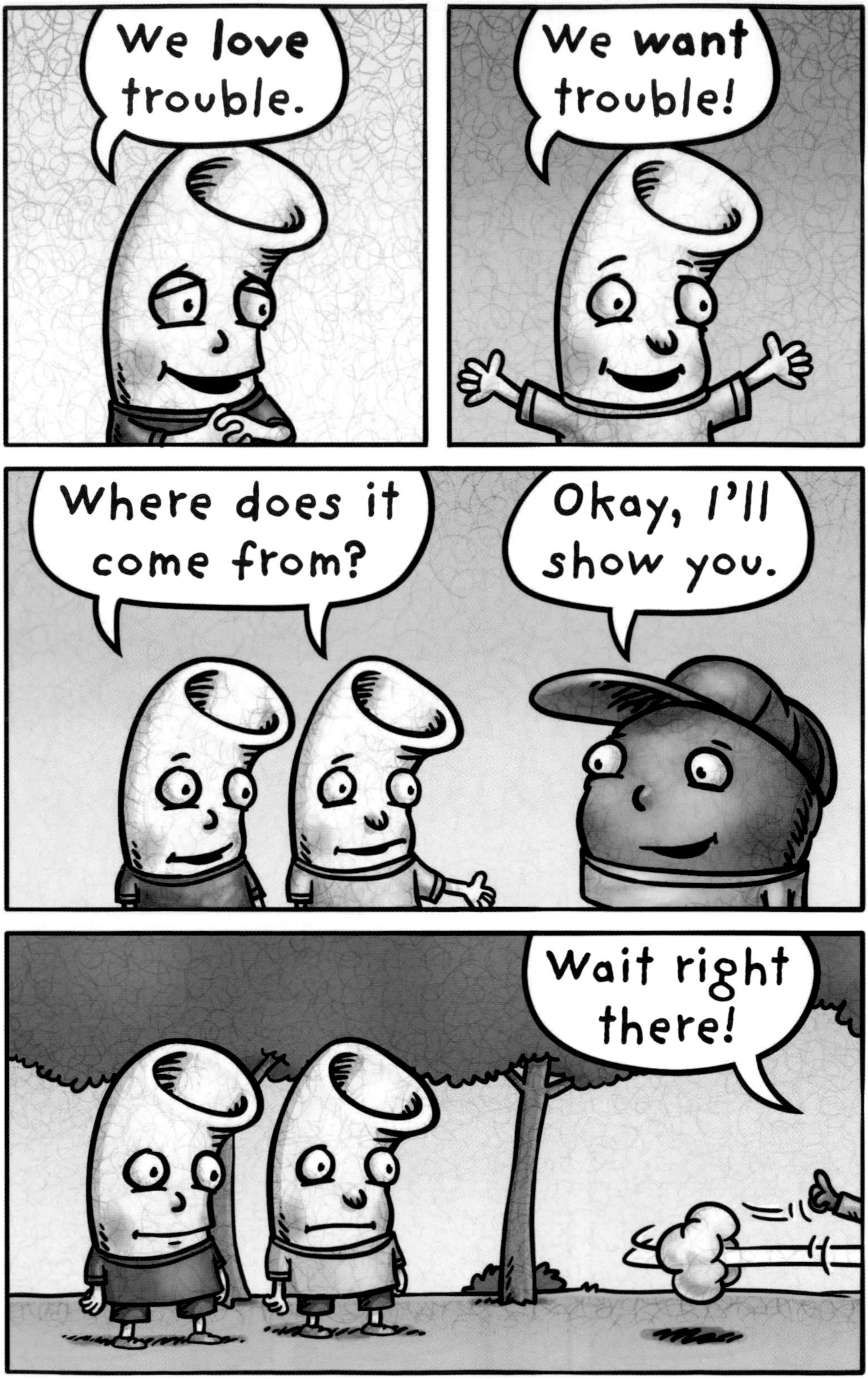
We love trouble.
We want trouble!
Where does it come from?
Okay, I'll show you.
Wait right there!

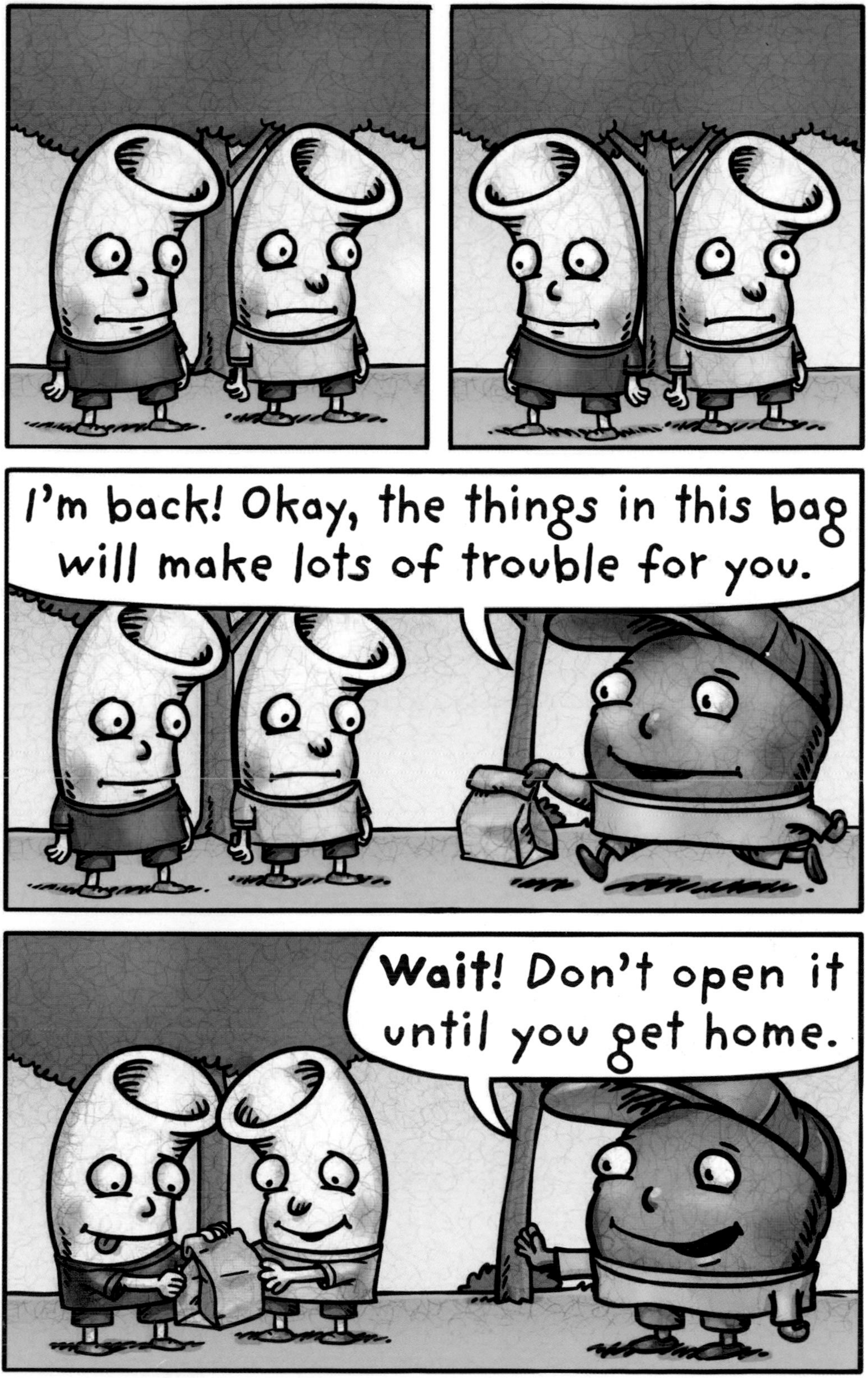
I'm back! Okay, the things in this bag will make lots of trouble for you.
Wait! Don't open it until you get home.

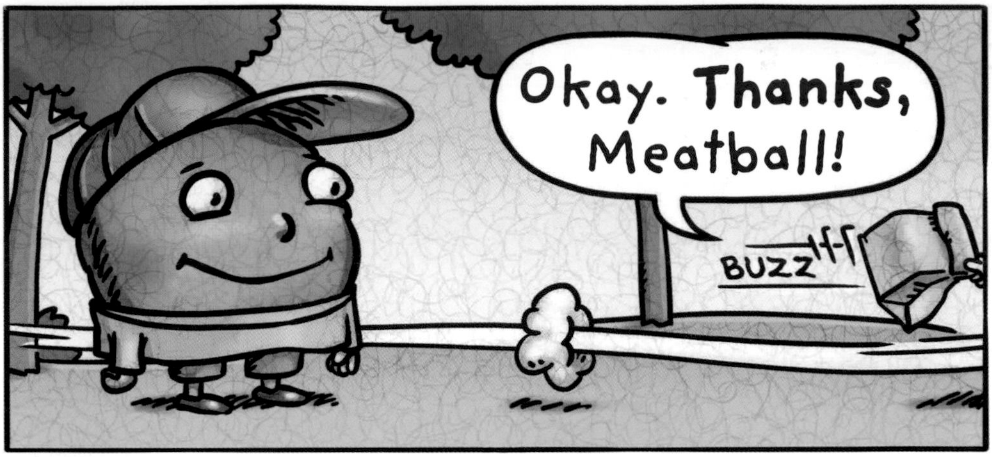
Okay. Thanks, Meatball!
BUZZ

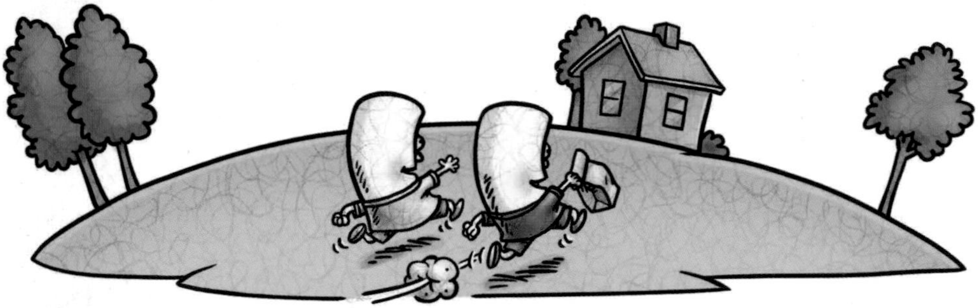

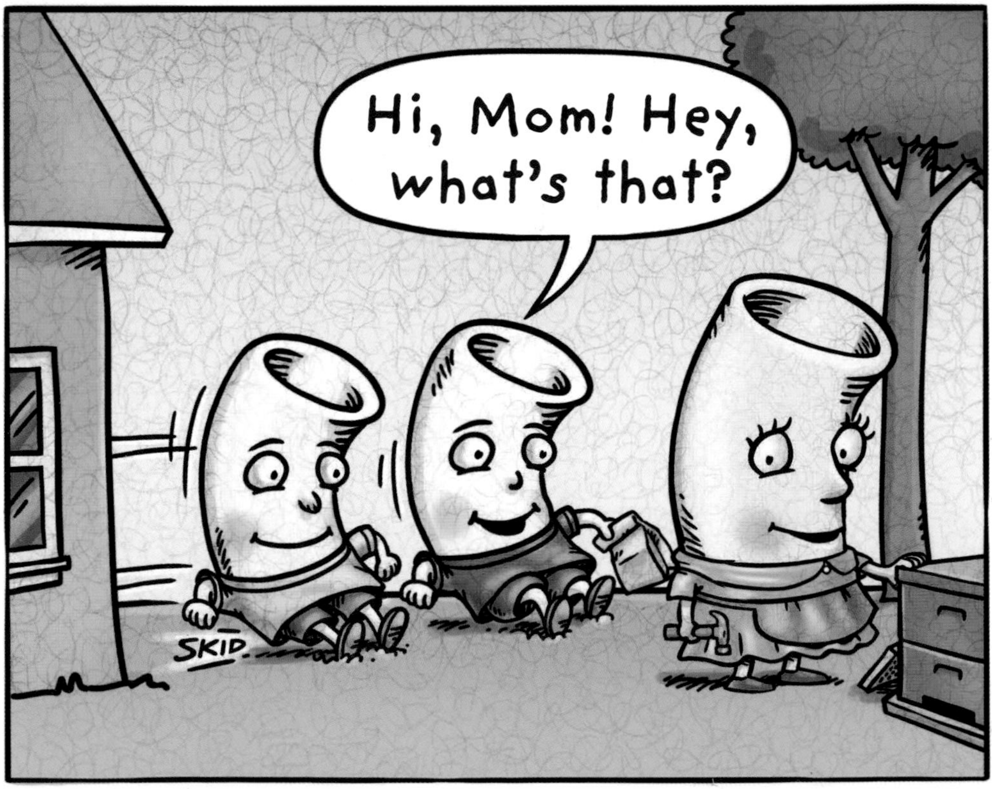
Hi, Mom! Hey, what's that?
SKID

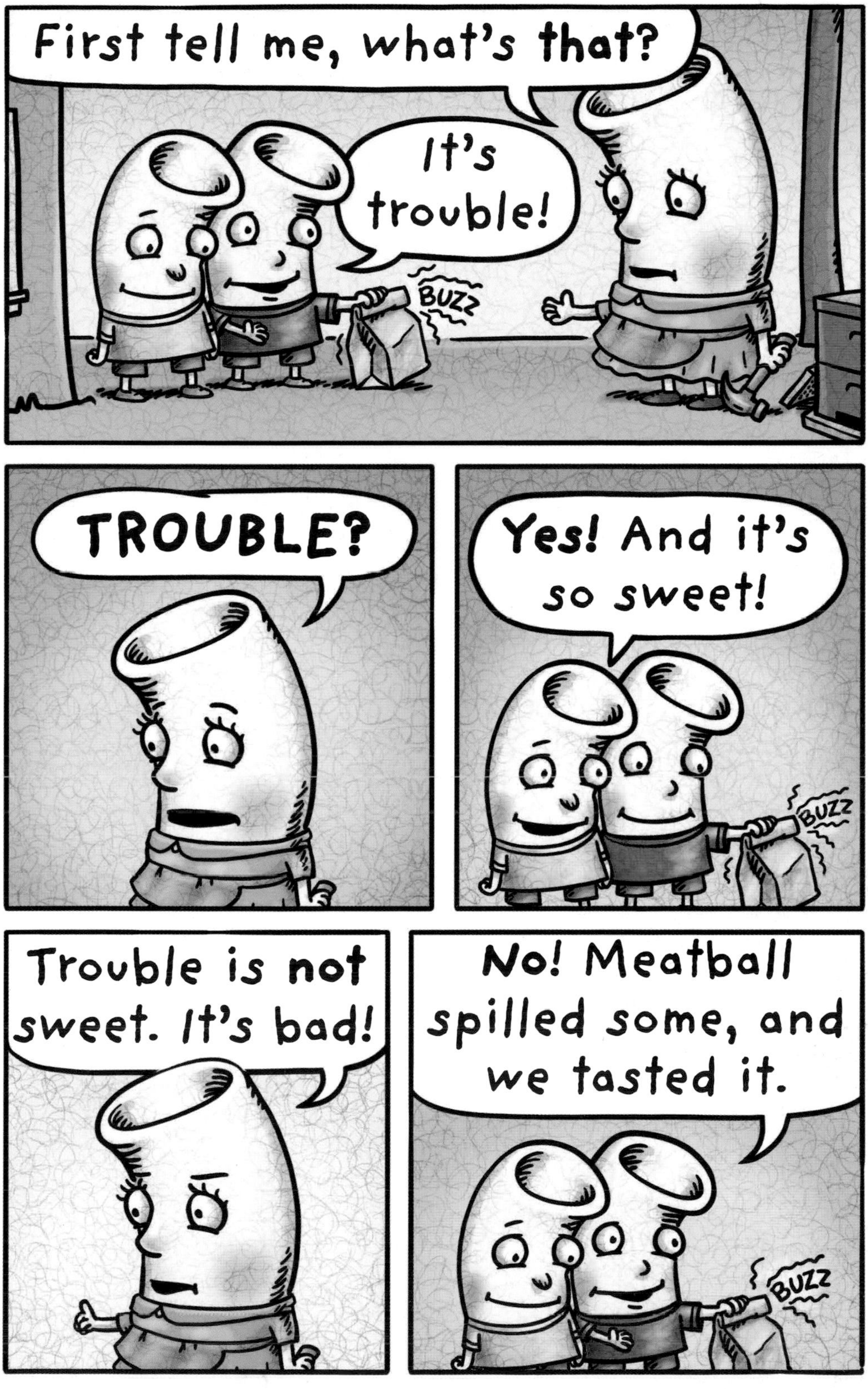

First tell me, what's that?
It's trouble!
BUZZ
TROUBLE?
Yes! And it's so sweet!
BUZZ
Trouble is not sweet. It's bad!
No! Meatball spilled some, and we tasted it.
BUZZ

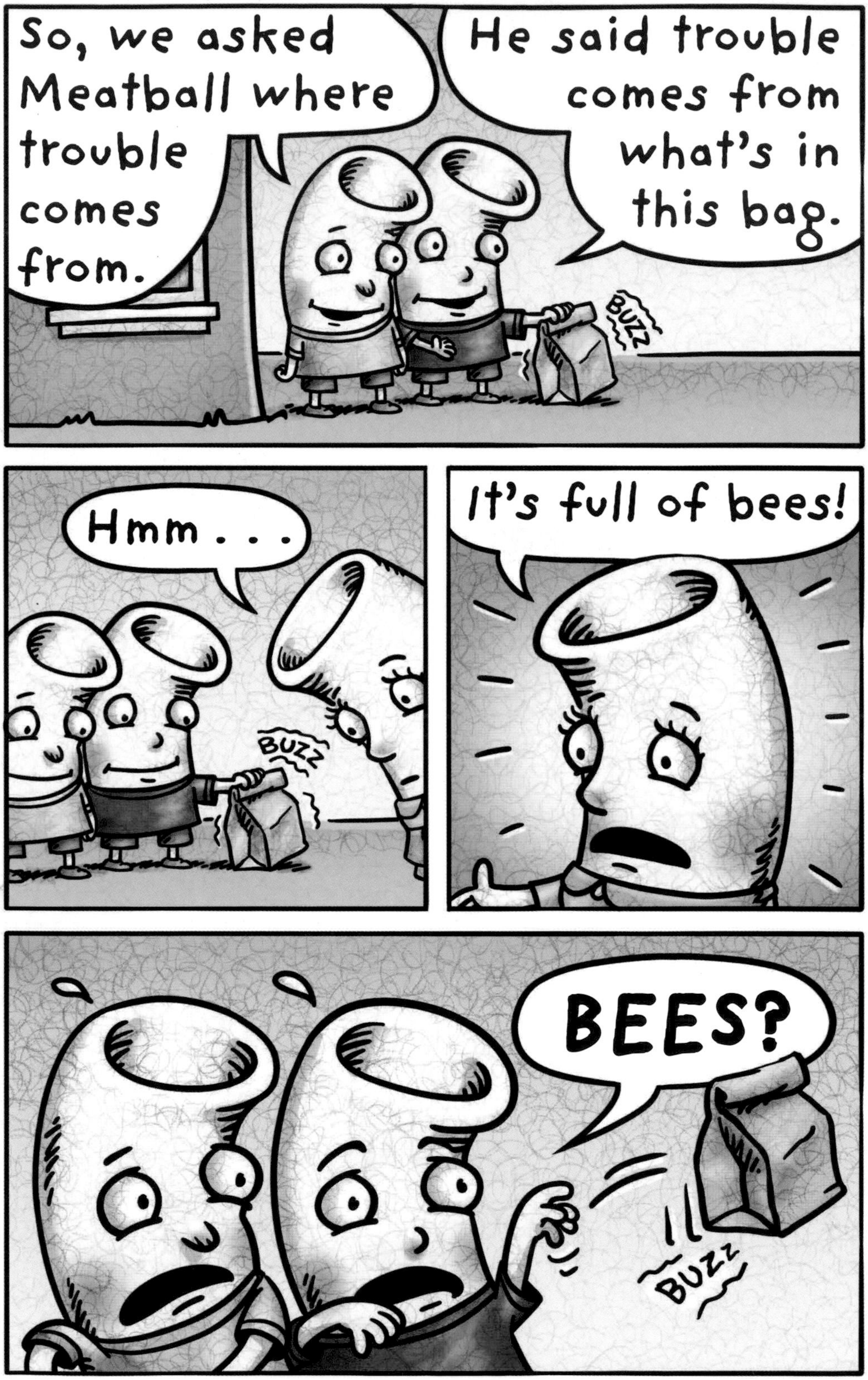
So, we asked Meatball where trouble comes from.
He said trouble comes from what's in this bag.
BUZZ
Hmm . . .
BUZZ
It's full of bees!
BEES?
BUZZ

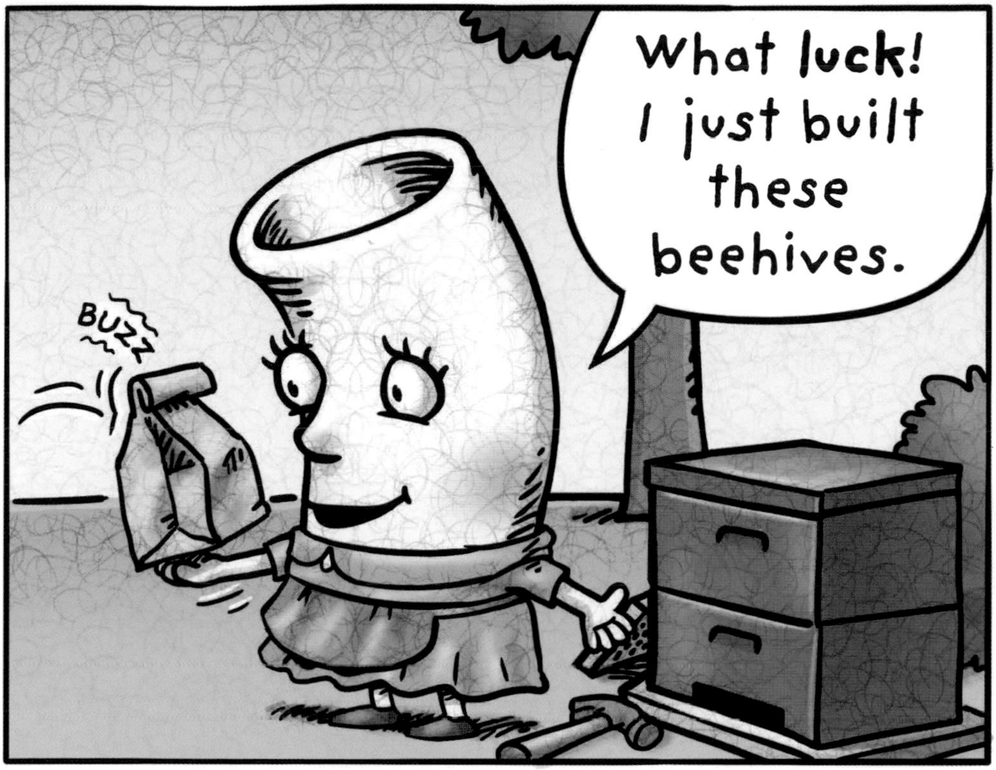
What luck! I just built these beehives.
BUZZ

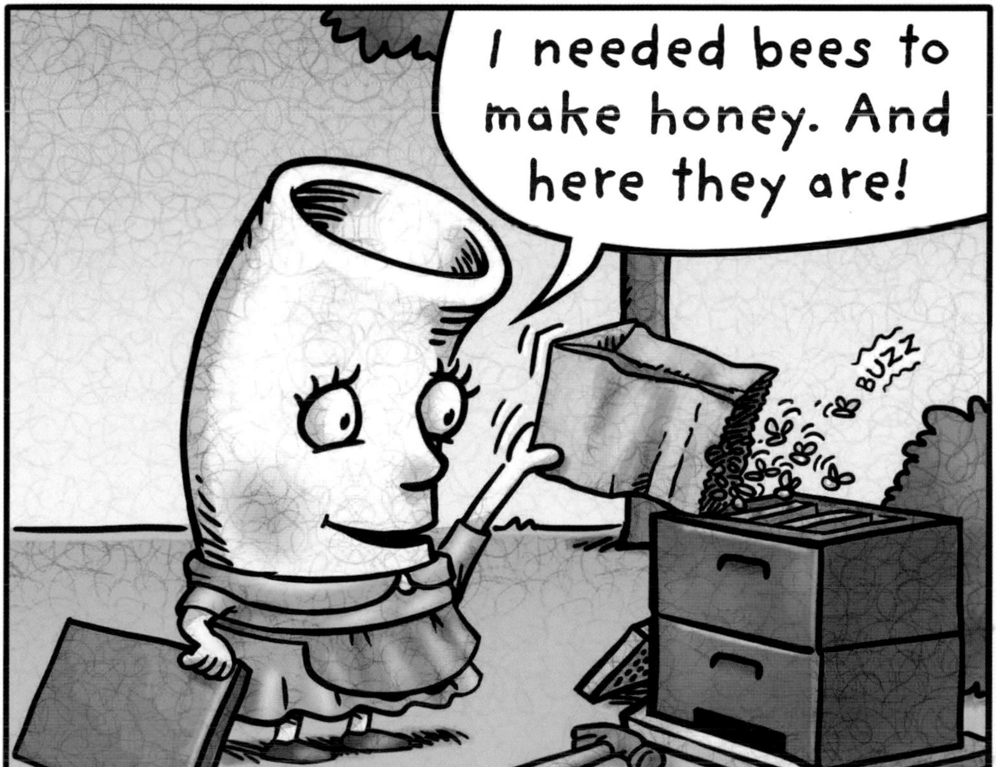
I needed bees to make honey. And here they are!
BUZZ

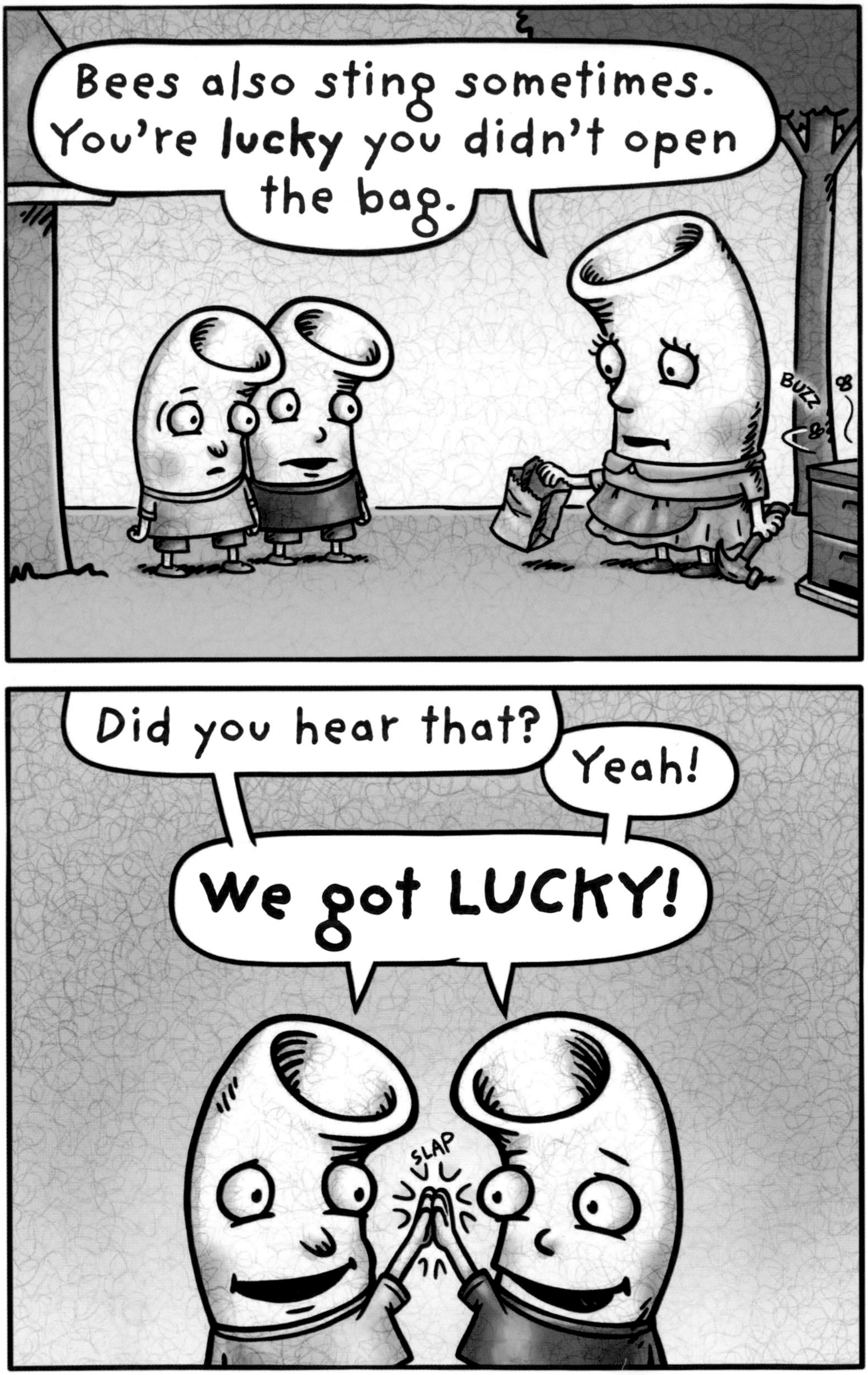
Bees also sting sometimes. You're lucky you didn't open the bag.
BUZZ
Did you hear that?
Yeah!
We got LUCKY!
SLAP

NOODLEHEADS LUCKY DAY

CHAPTER 2

HOW TO HATCH A CAT

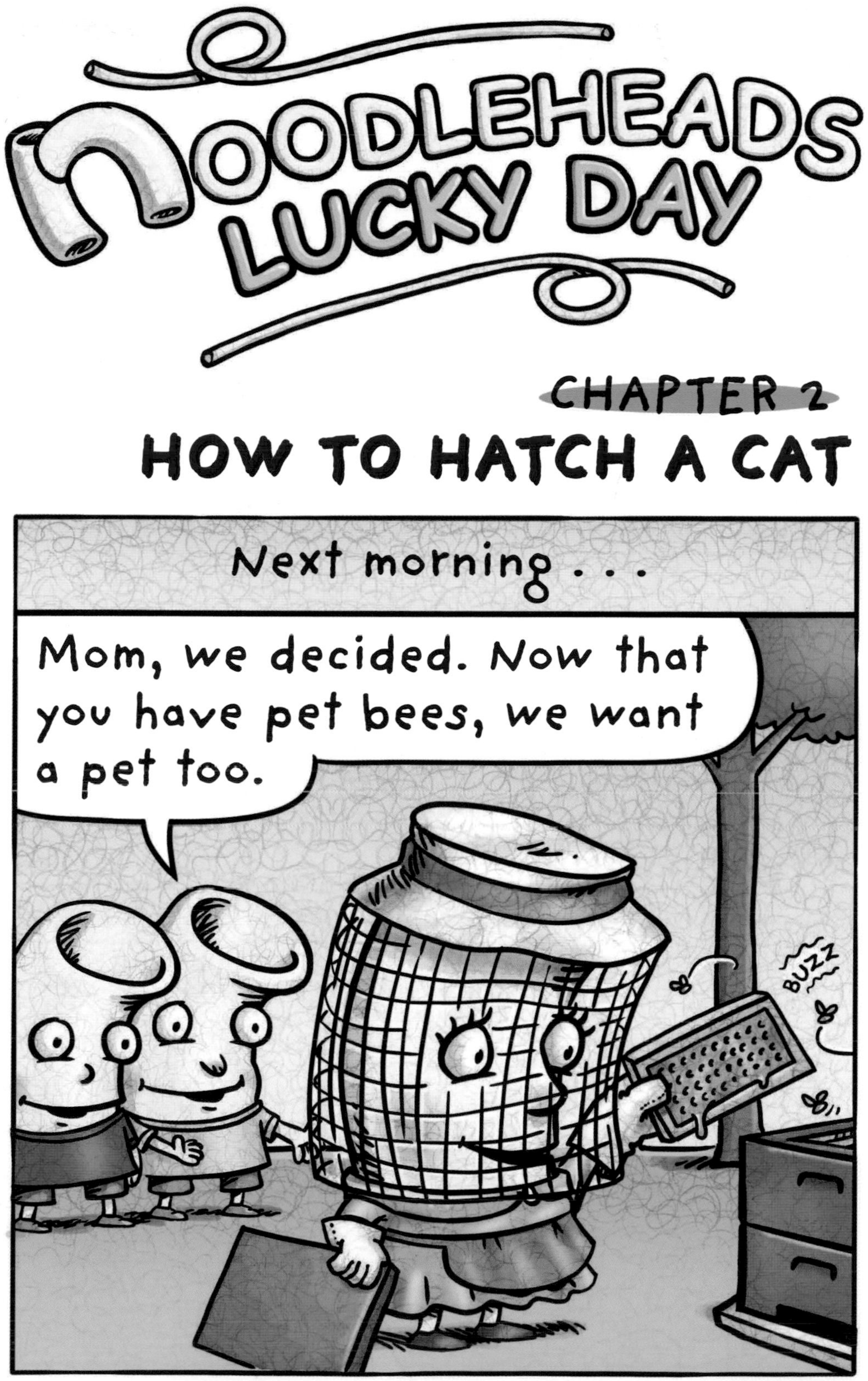
Next morning . . .
Mom, we decided. Now that you have pet bees, we want a pet too.
BUZZ

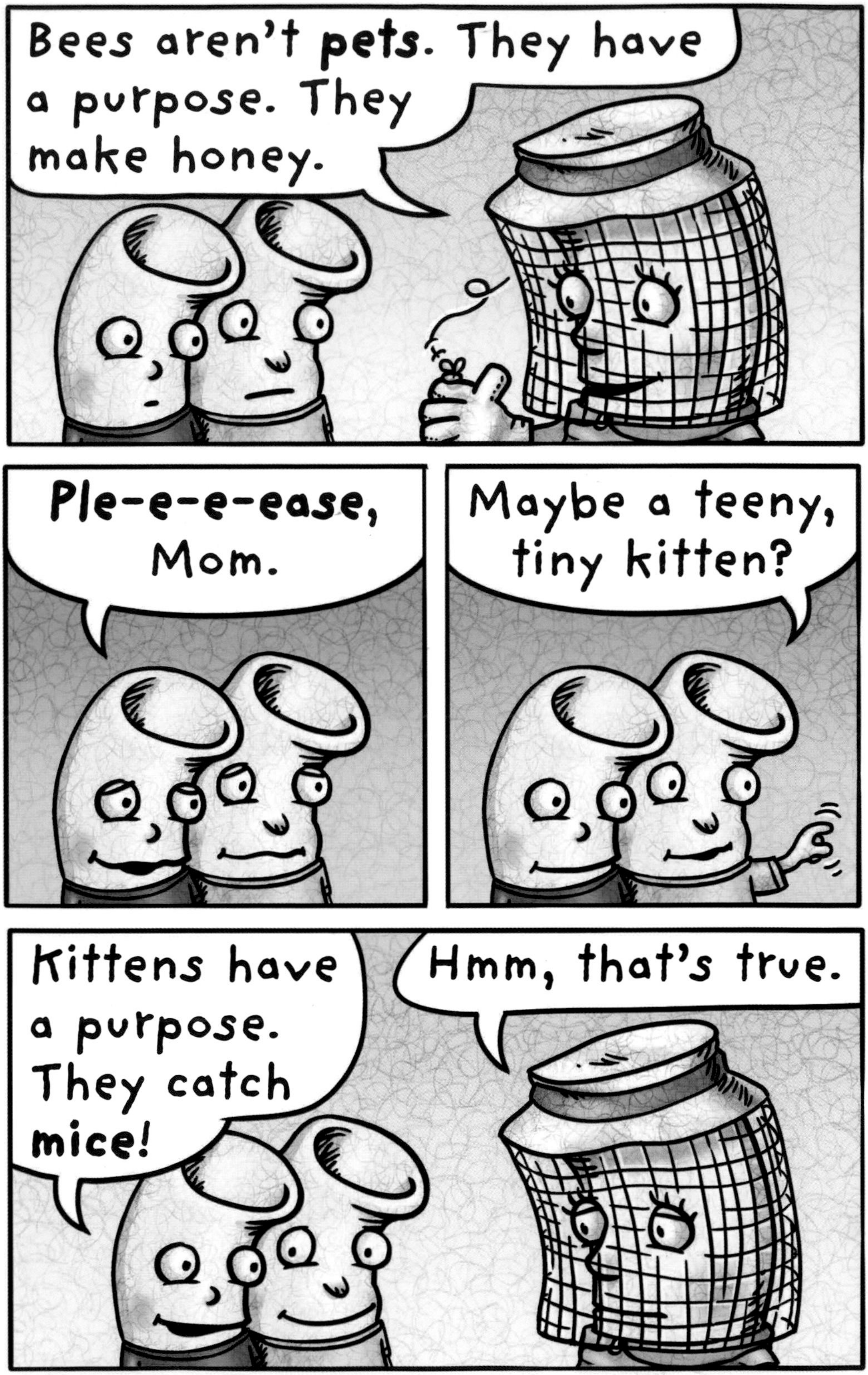
Bees aren't pets. They have a purpose. They make honey.
Ple-e-e-ease, Mom.
Maybe a teeny, tiny kitten?
Kittens have a purpose. They catch mice!
Hmm, that's true.

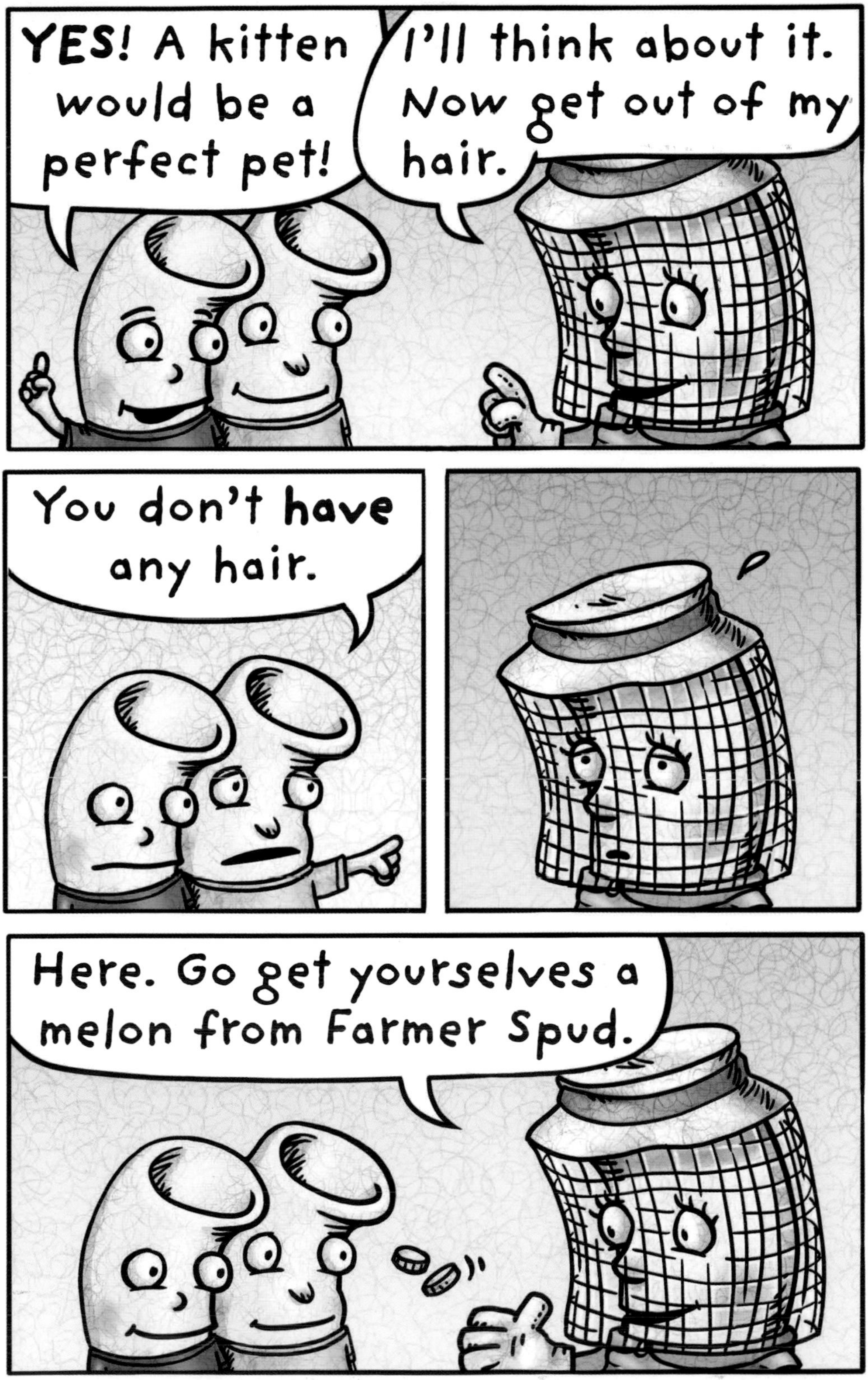
YES! A kitten would be a perfect pet!
I'll think about it. Now get out of my hair.
You don't have any hair.
Here. Go get yourselves a melon from Farmer Spud.

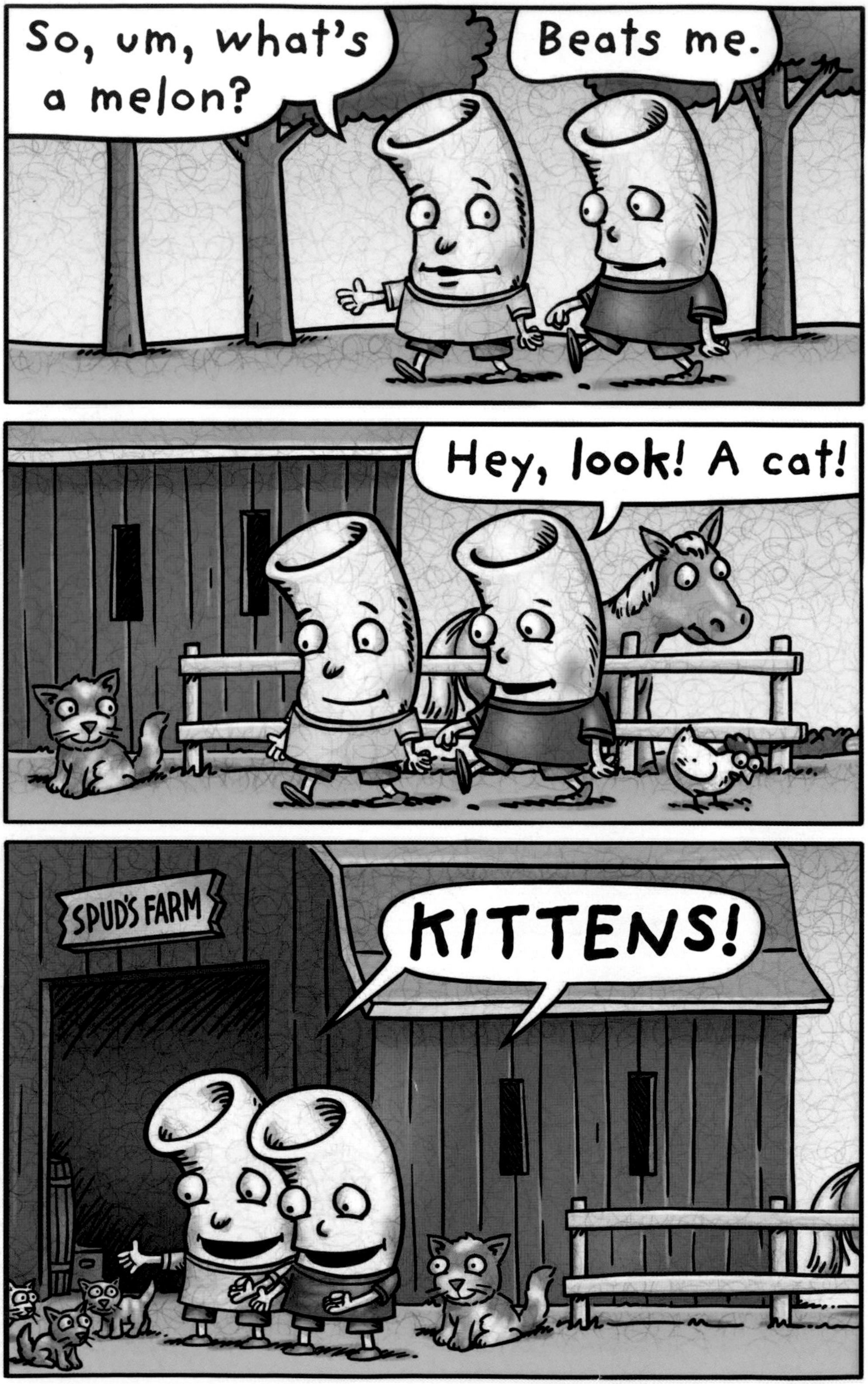
So, um, what's a melon?
Beats me.
Hey, look! A cat!
SPUD'S FARM
KITTENS!

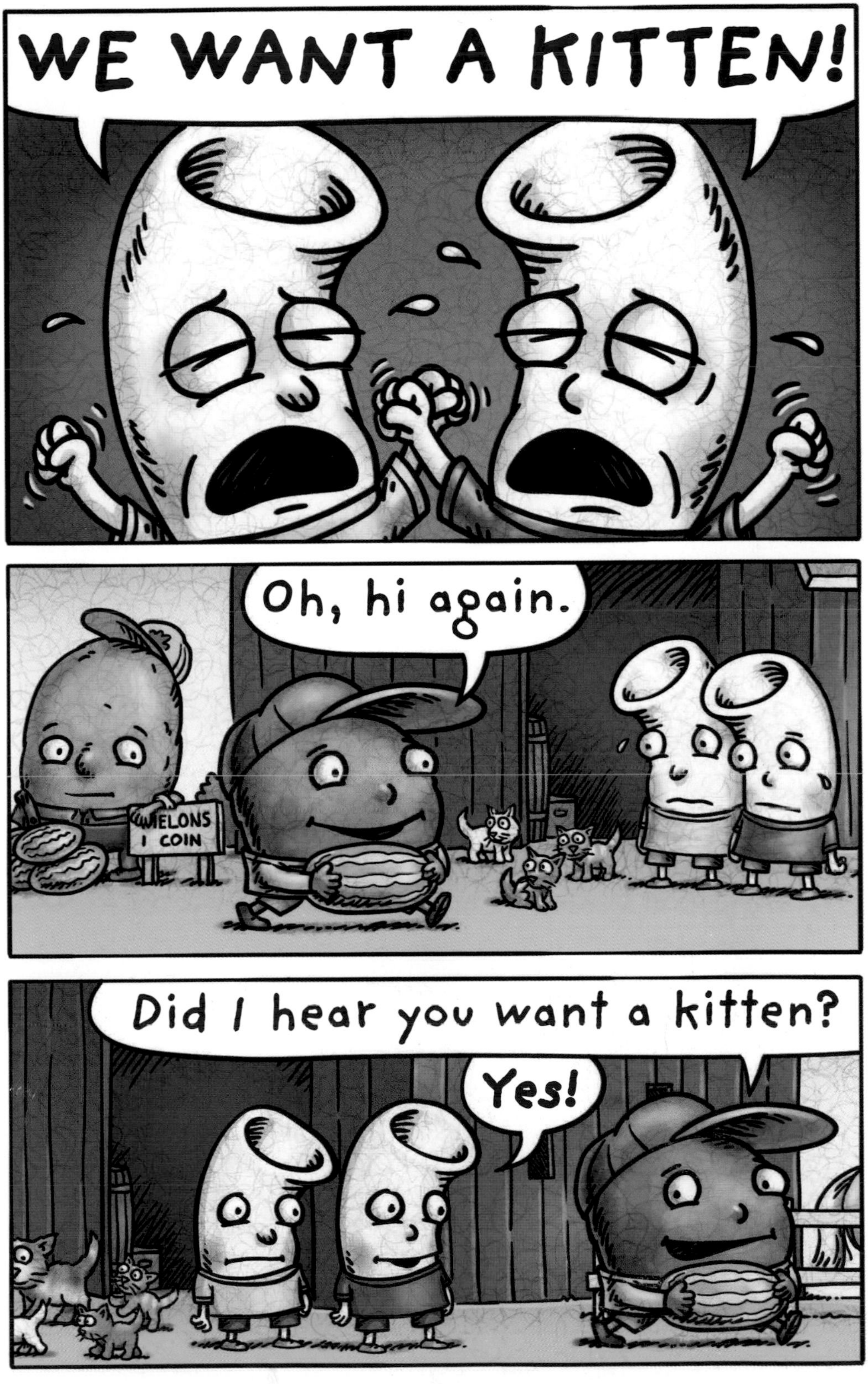
WE WANT A KITTEN!
Oh, hi again.
MELONS
1 COIN
Did I hear you want a kitten?
Yes!

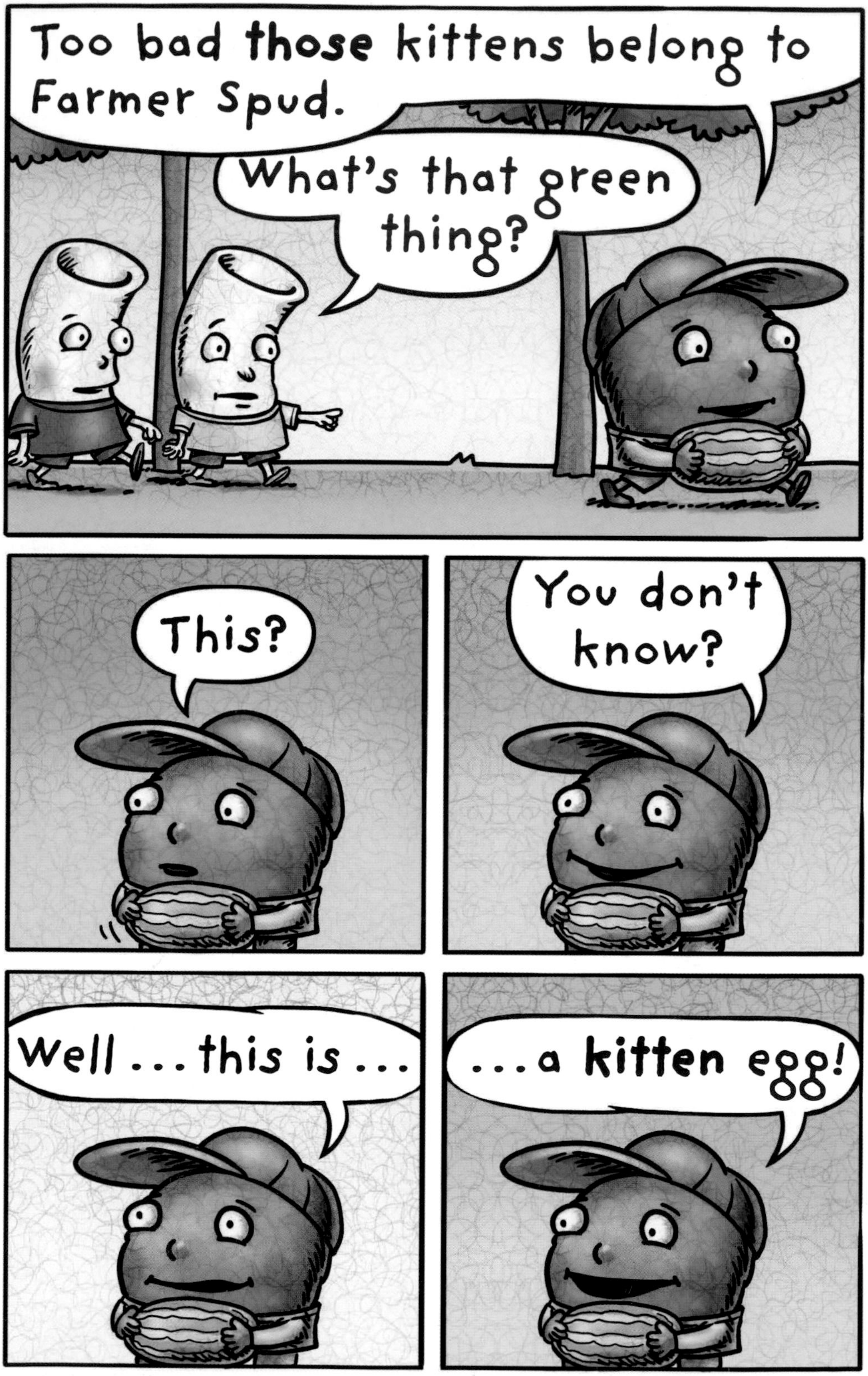
Too bad those kittens belong to Farmer Spud.
What's that green thing?
This?
You don't know?
Well . . . this is . . .
. . . a kitten egg!

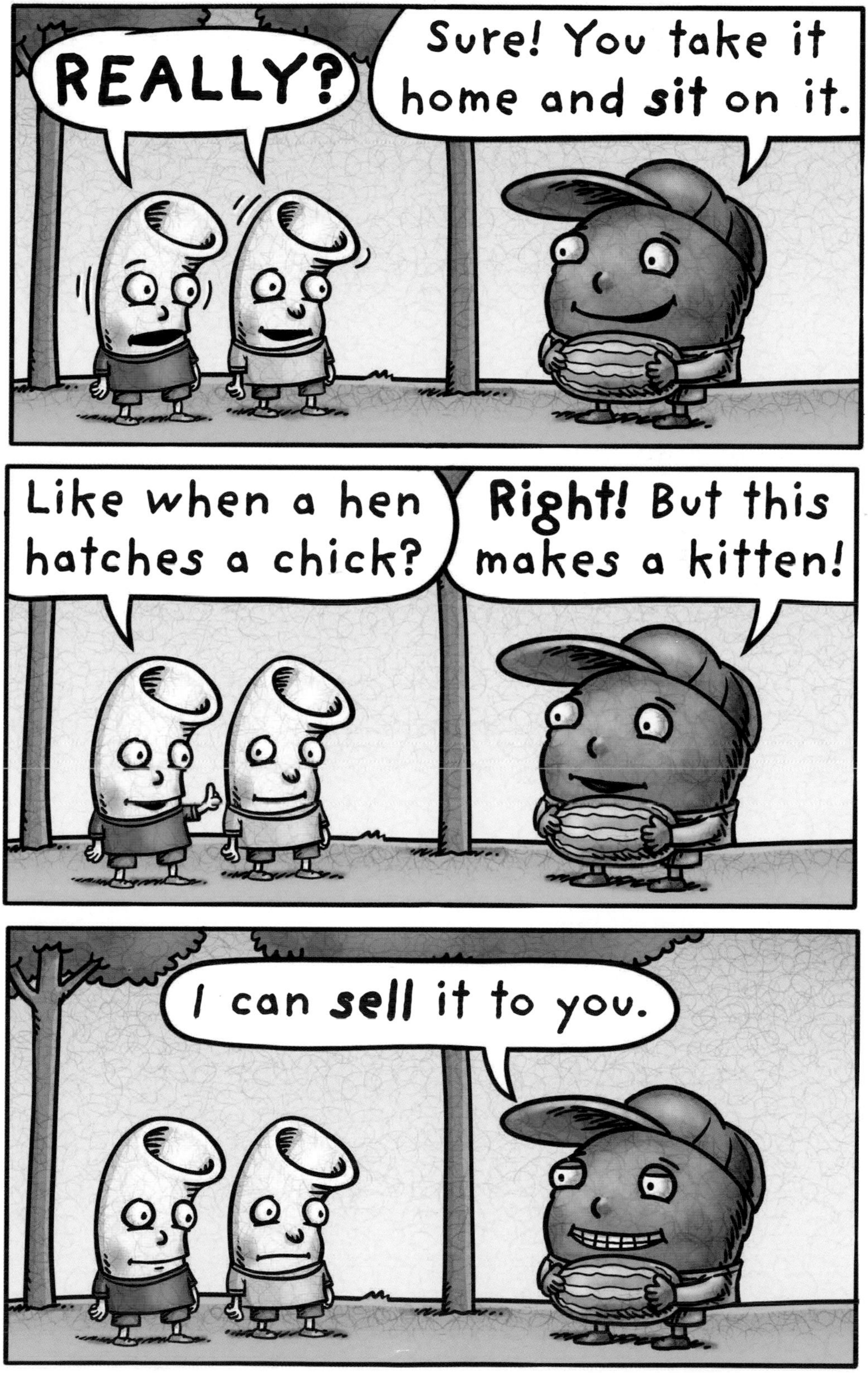
REALLY?
Sure! You take it home and **sit** on it.
Like when a hen hatches a chick?
Right! But this makes a kitten!
I can **sell** it to you.

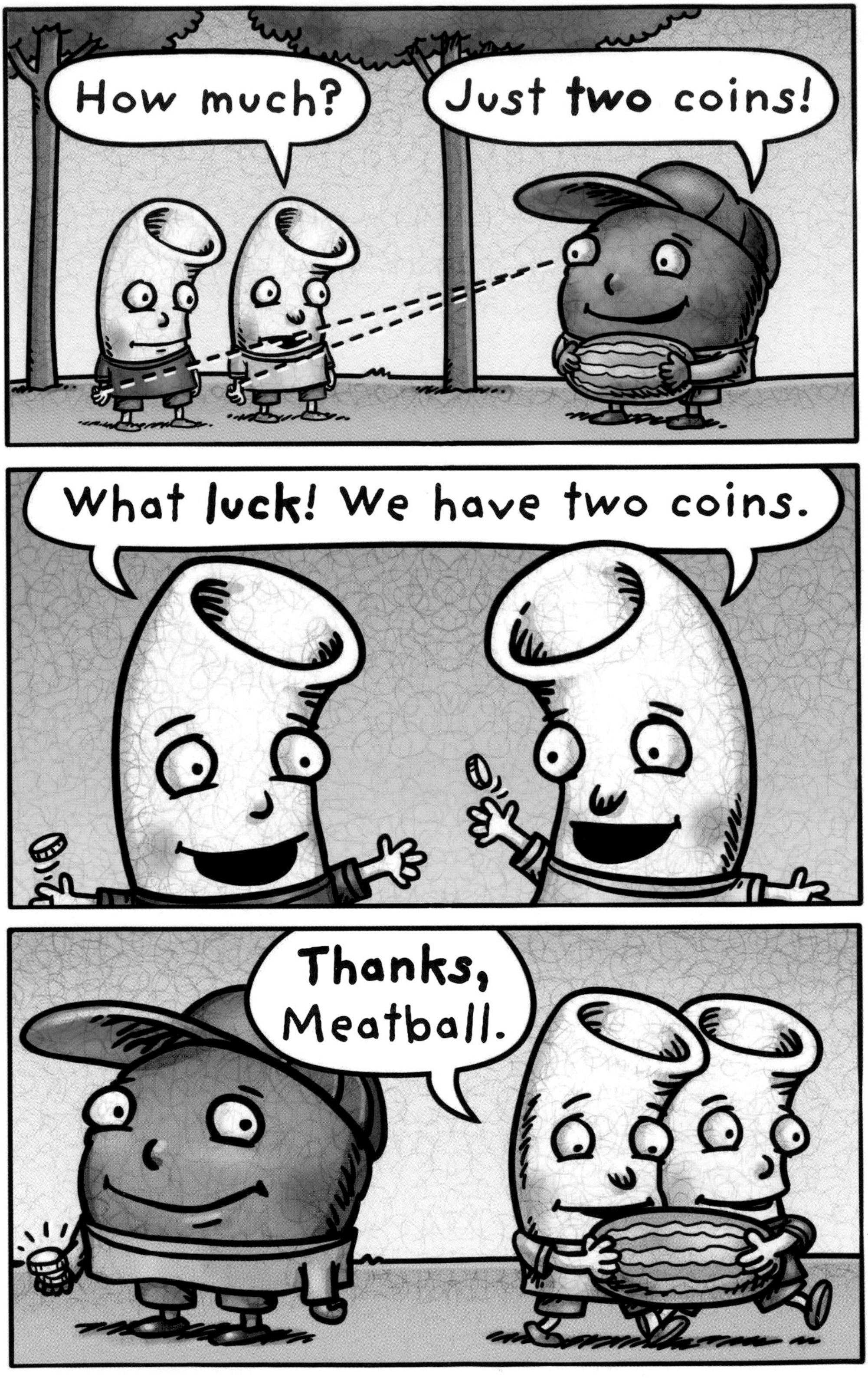
How much?
Just two coins!
What luck! We have two coins.
Thanks, Meatball.

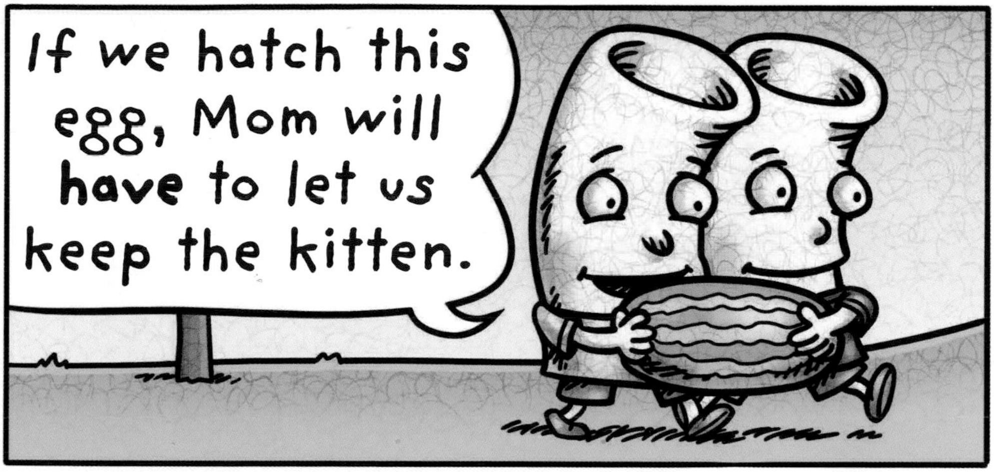
If we hatch this egg, Mom will have to let us keep the kitten.

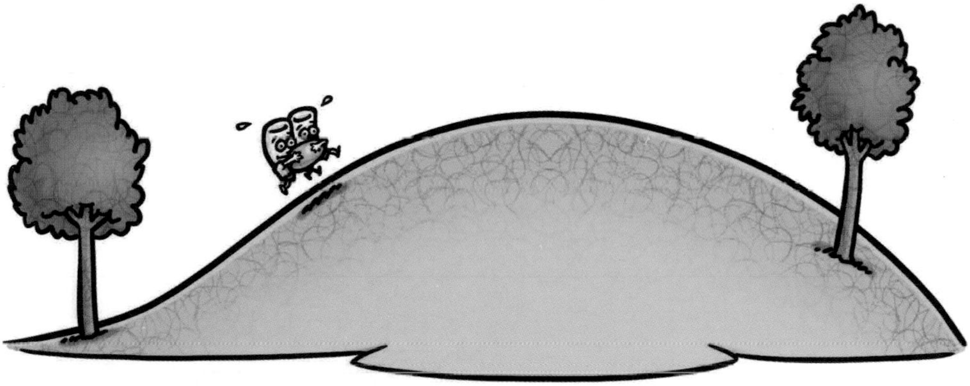

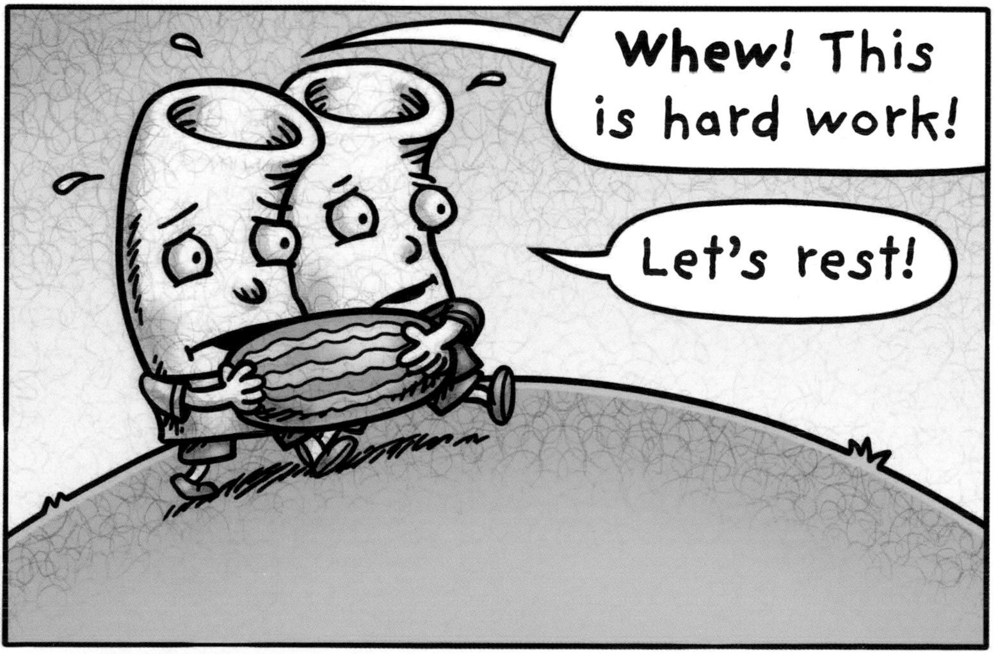
Whew! This is hard work!
Let's rest!

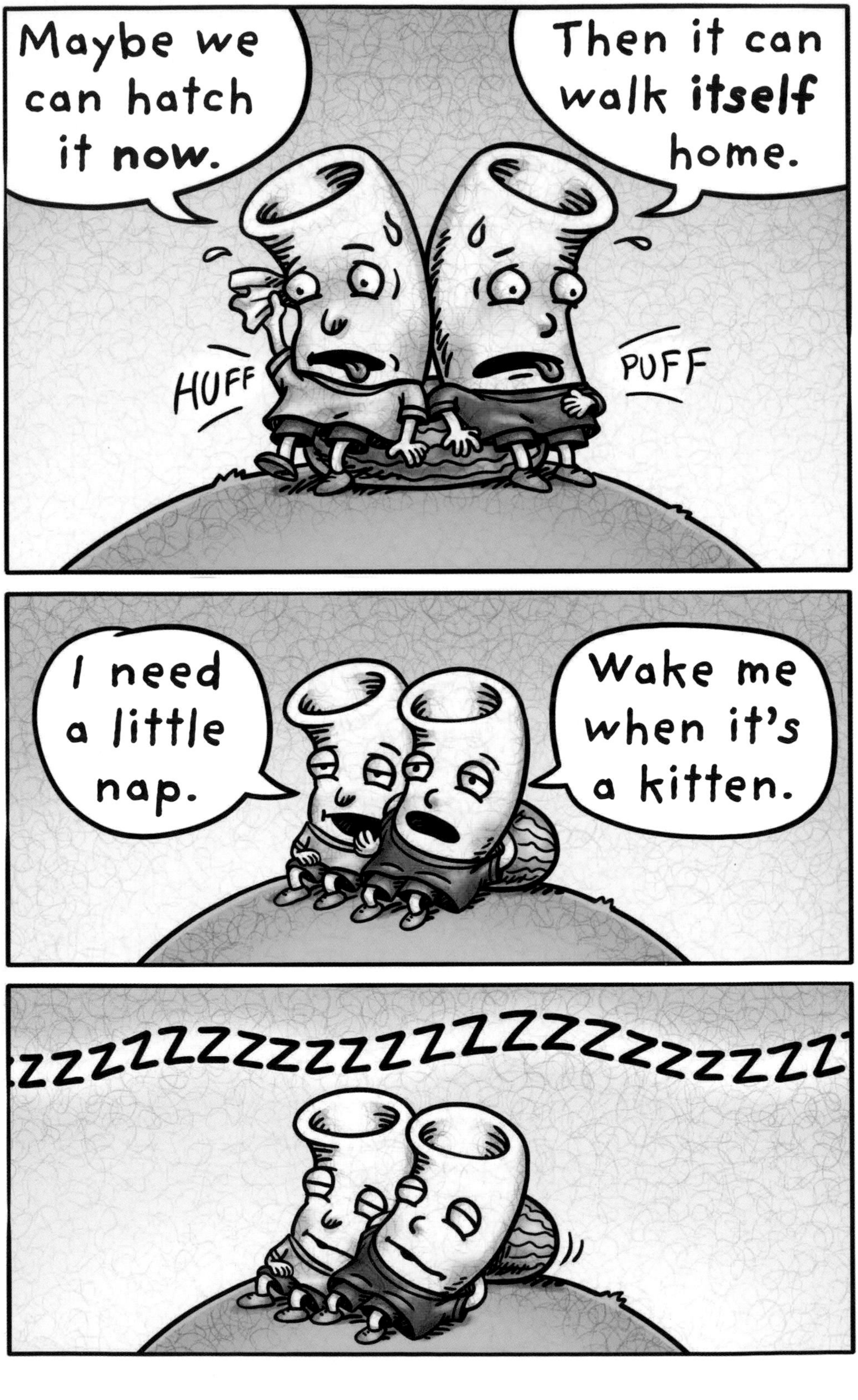
Maybe we can hatch it now.
Then it can walk **itself** home.
HUFF
PUFF
I need a little nap.
Wake me when it's a kitten.
ZZZZZZZZZZZZZZZZZZZZZZZZZZZ

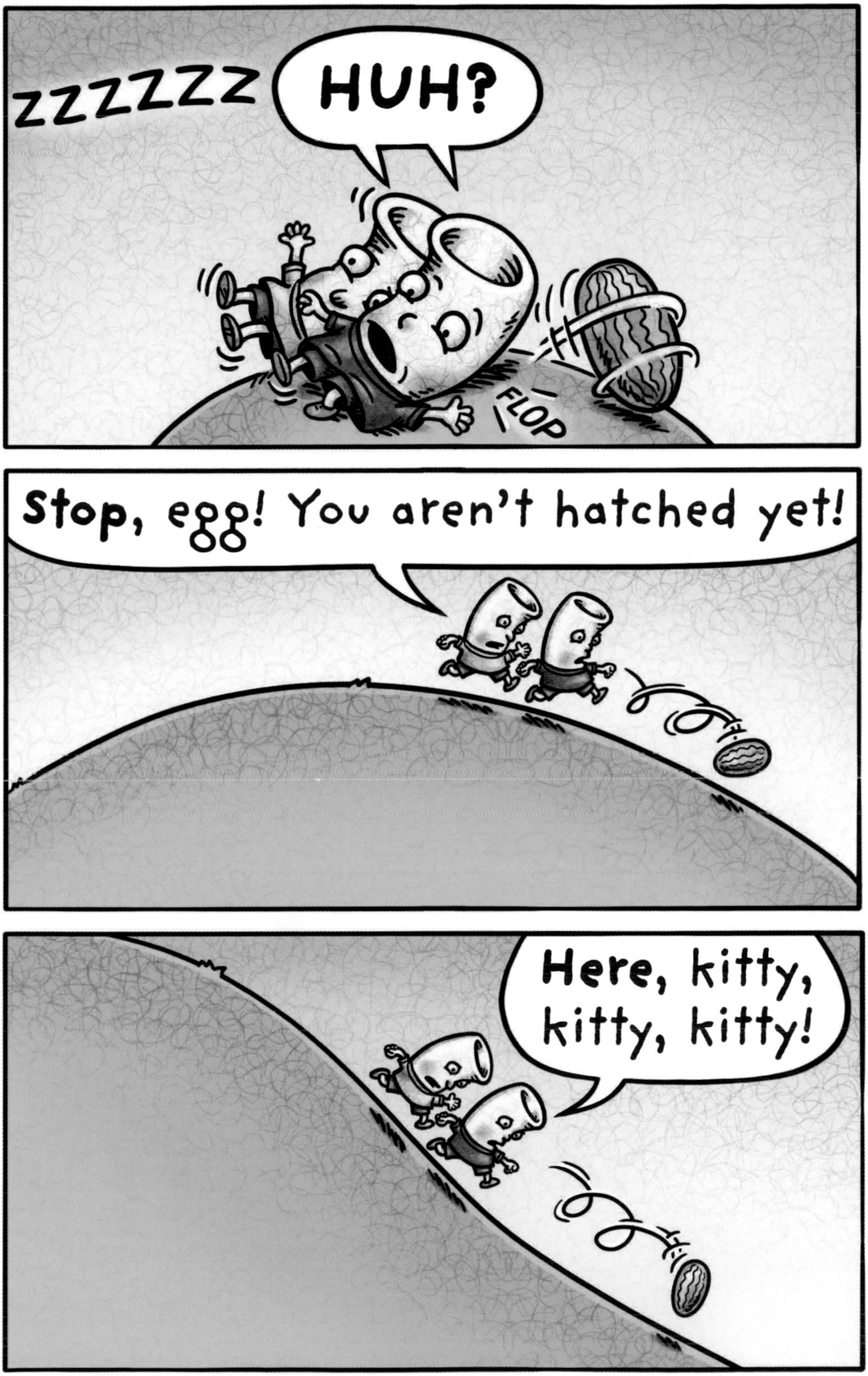
ZZZZZZ
HUH?
FLOP
Stop, egg! You aren't hatched yet!
Here, kitty, kitty, kitty, kitty!

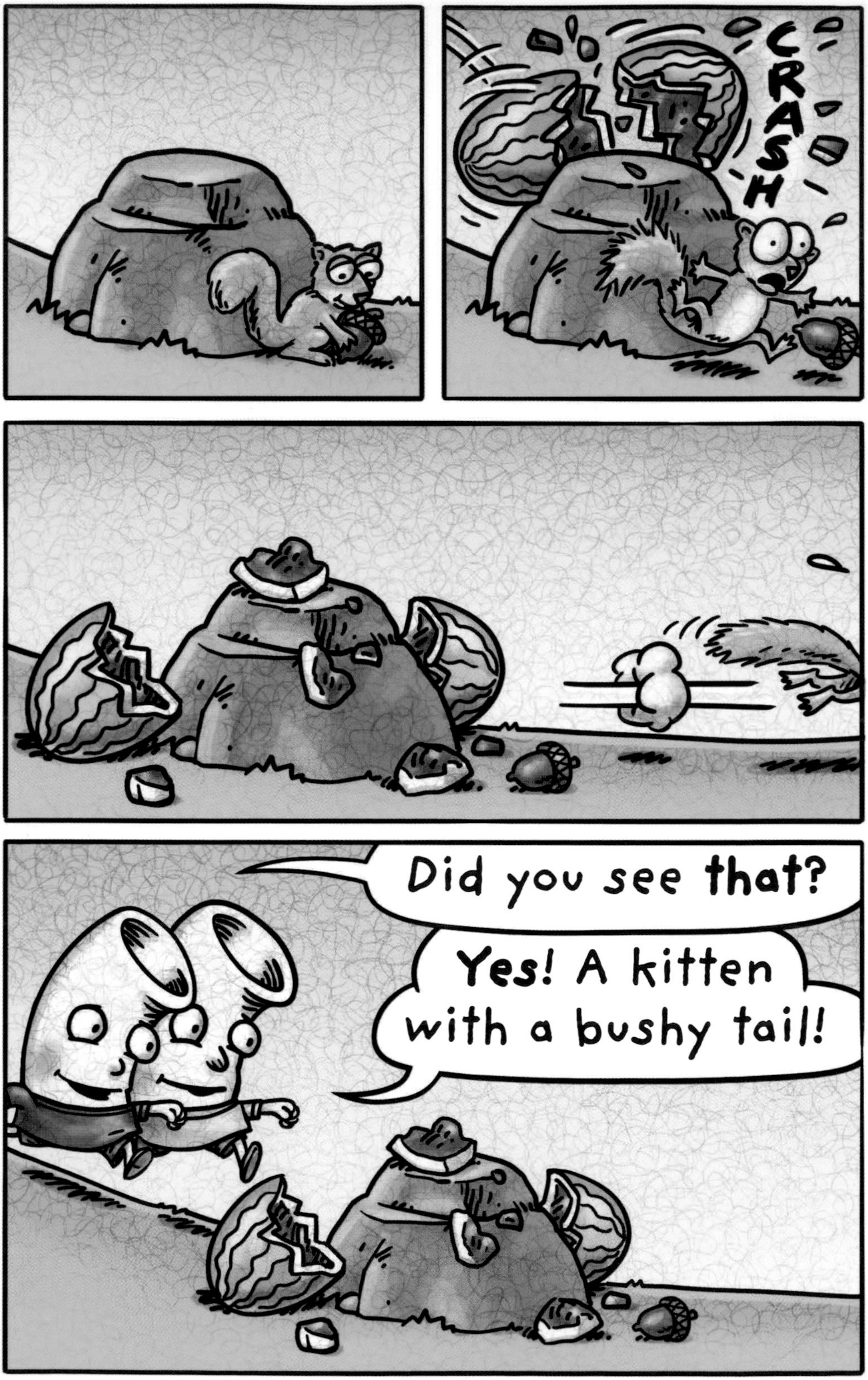
CRASH
Did you see that?
Yes! A kitten with a bushy tail!

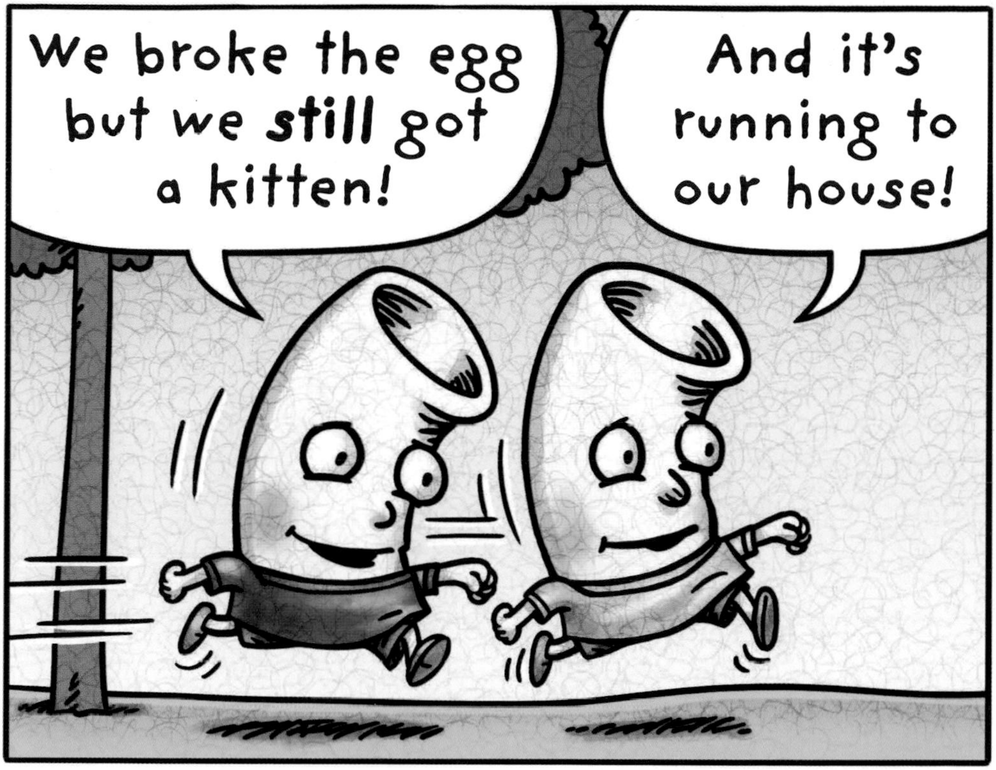
We broke the egg but we still got a kitten!
And it's running to our house!

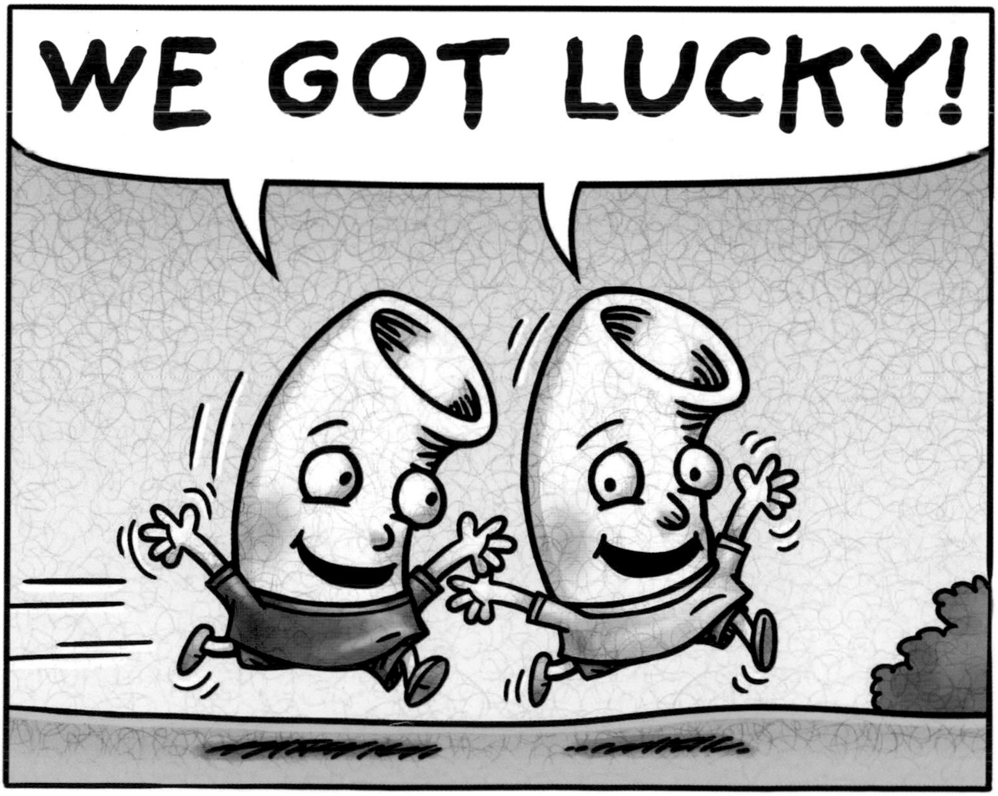
WE GOT LUCKY!

NOODLEHEADS LUCKY DAY

CHAPTER 3

THE PERFECT NAME

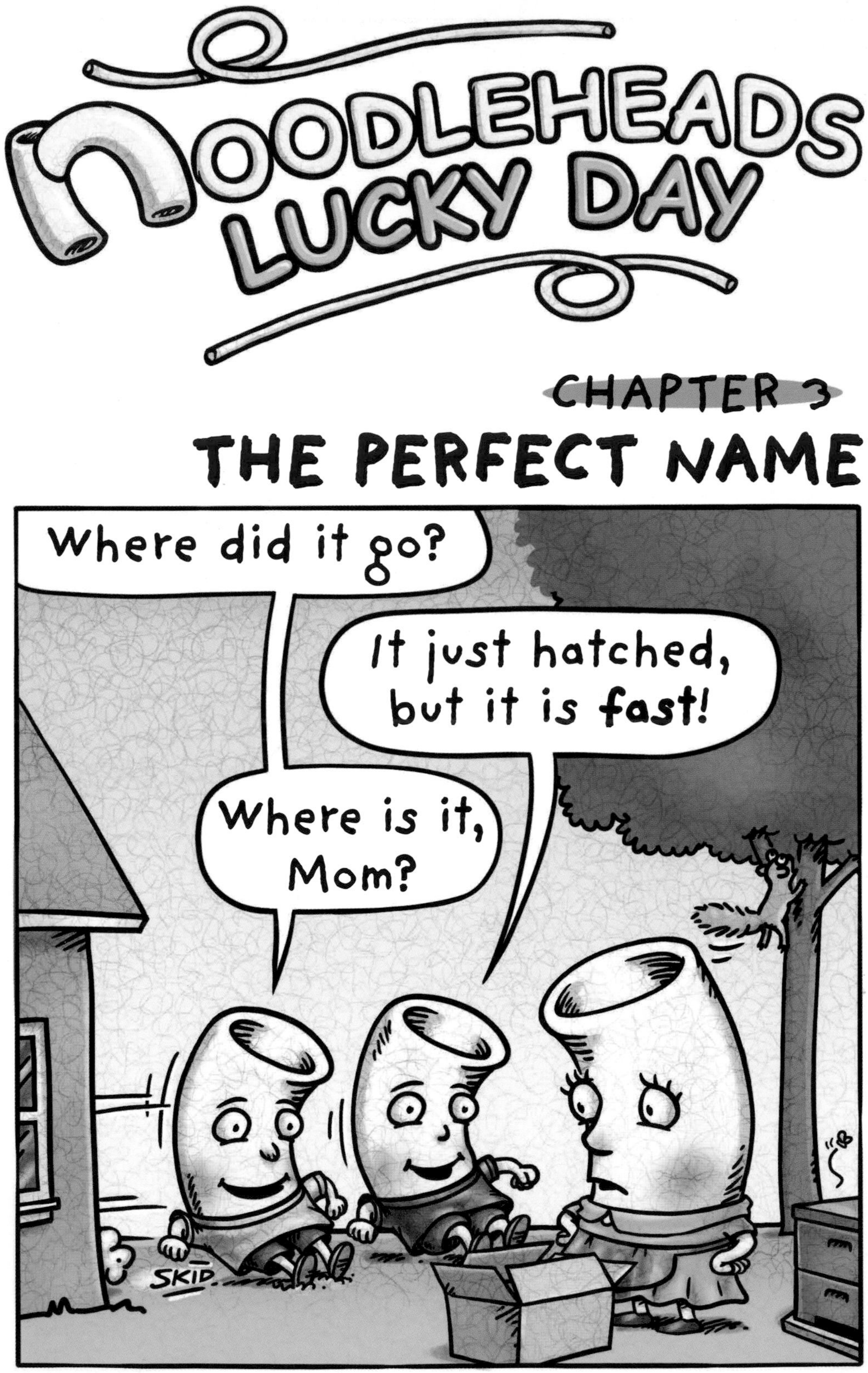
Where did it go?
It just hatched, but it is **fast**!
Where is it, Mom?
SKID

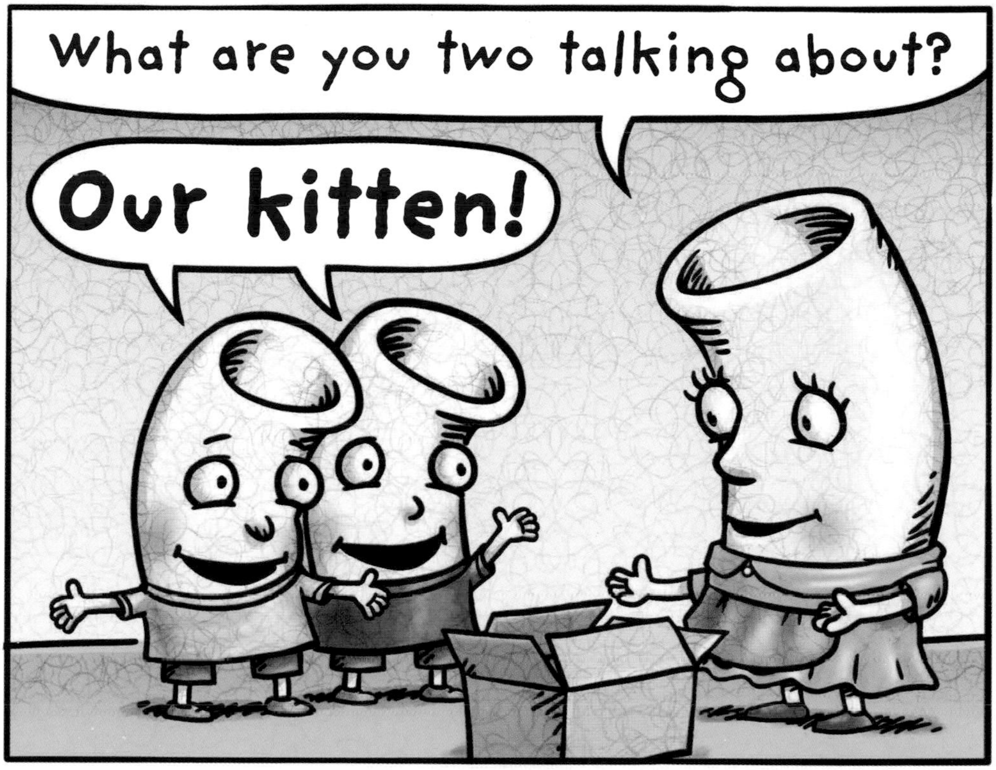
What are you two talking about?
Our kitten!

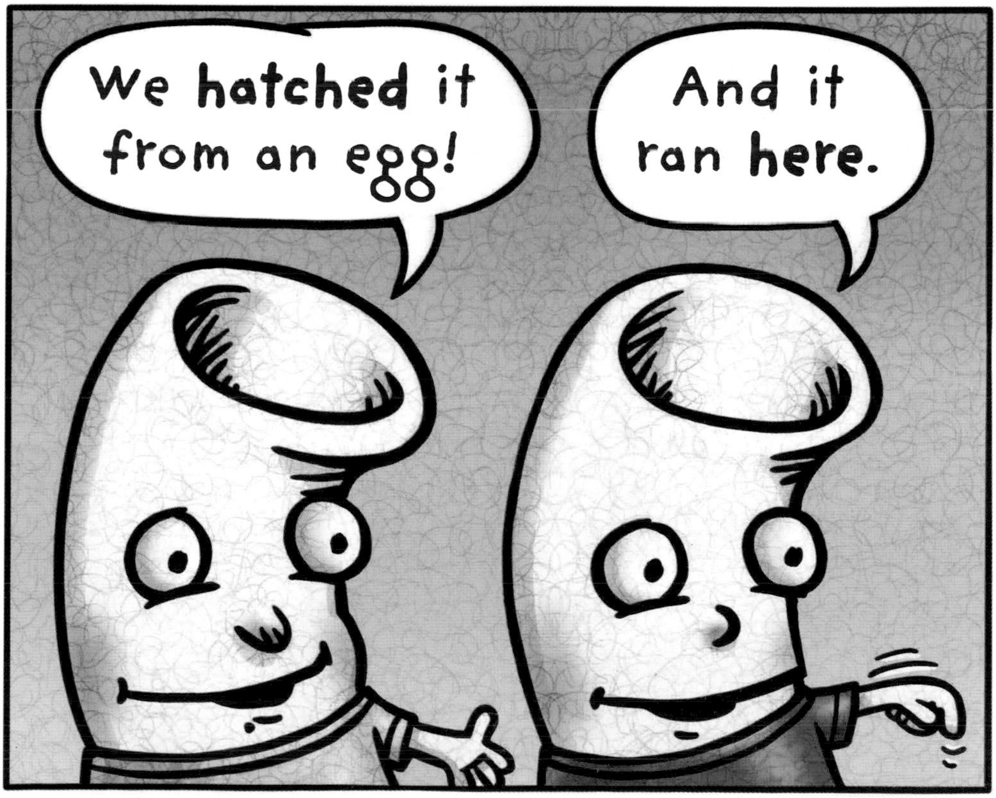
We hatched it from an egg!
And it ran here.

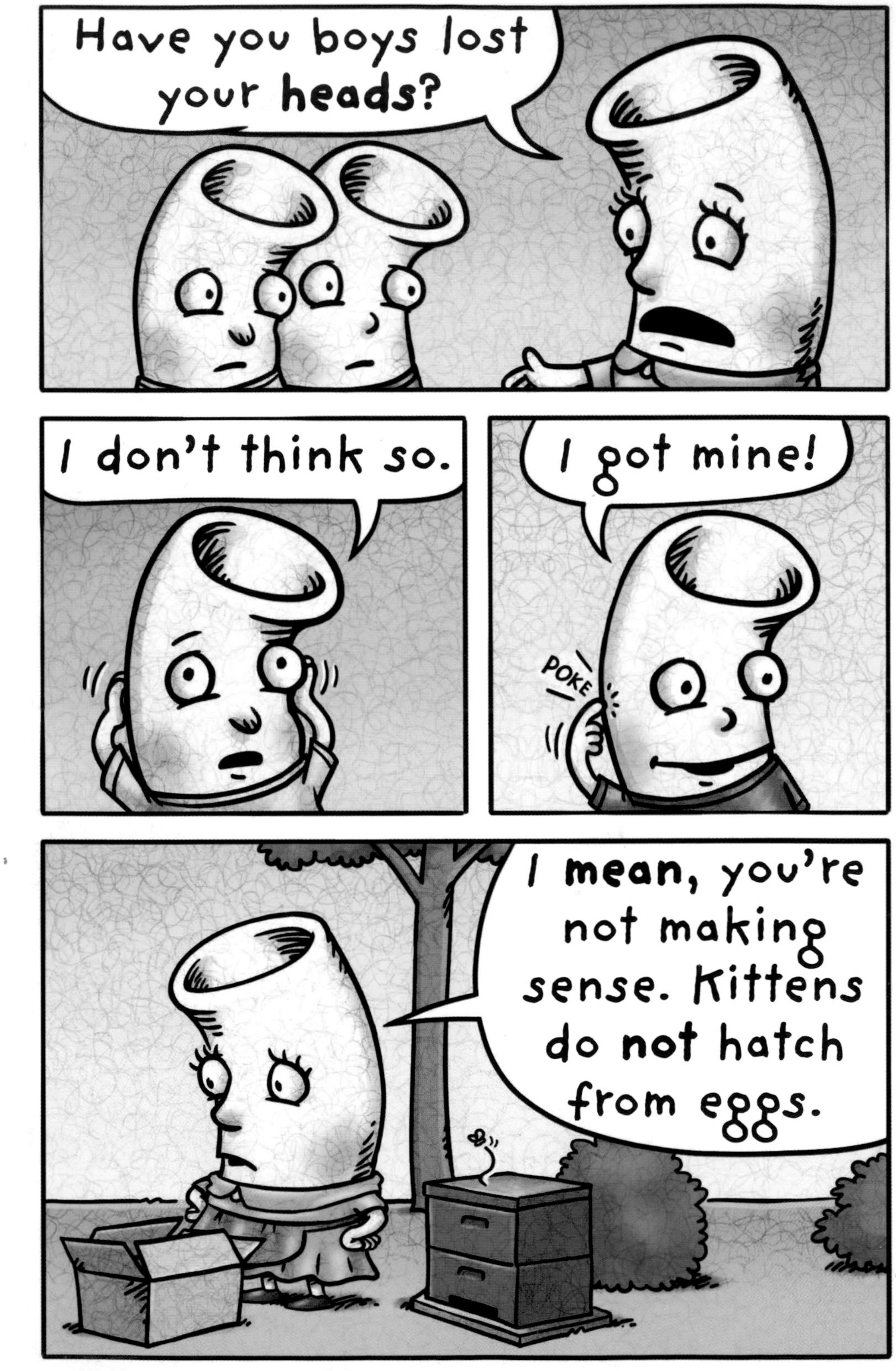
Have you boys lost your **heads**?
I don't think so.
I got mine!
POKE
I **mean**, you're not making sense. Kittens do **not** hatch from eggs.

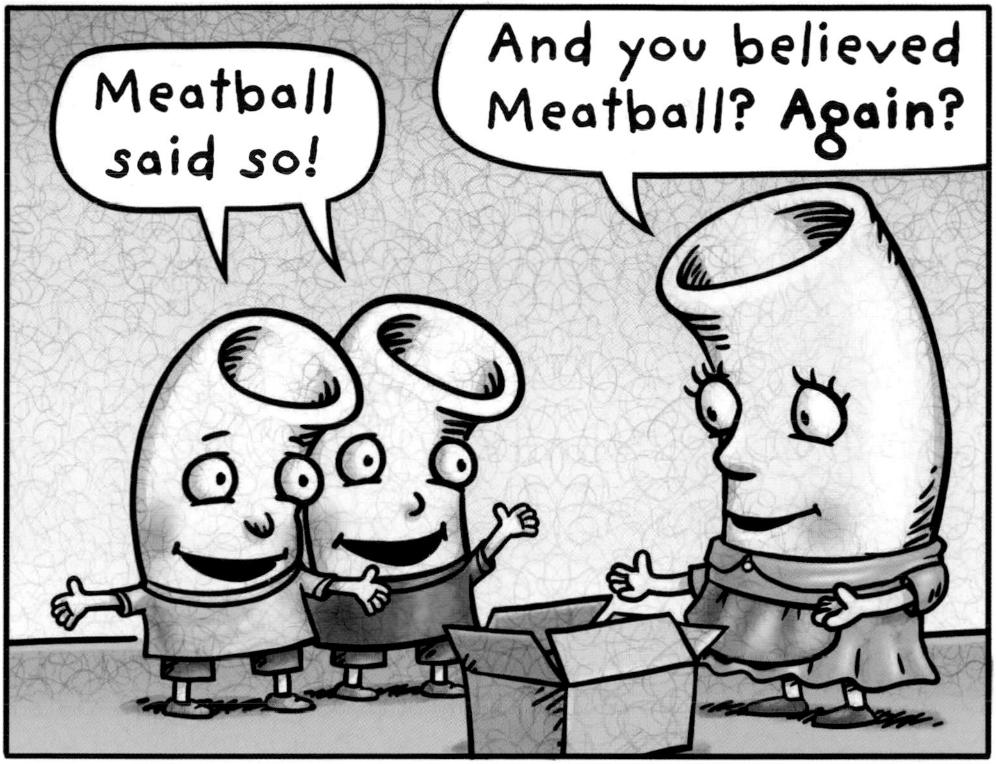
Meatball said so!
And you believed Meatball? Again?

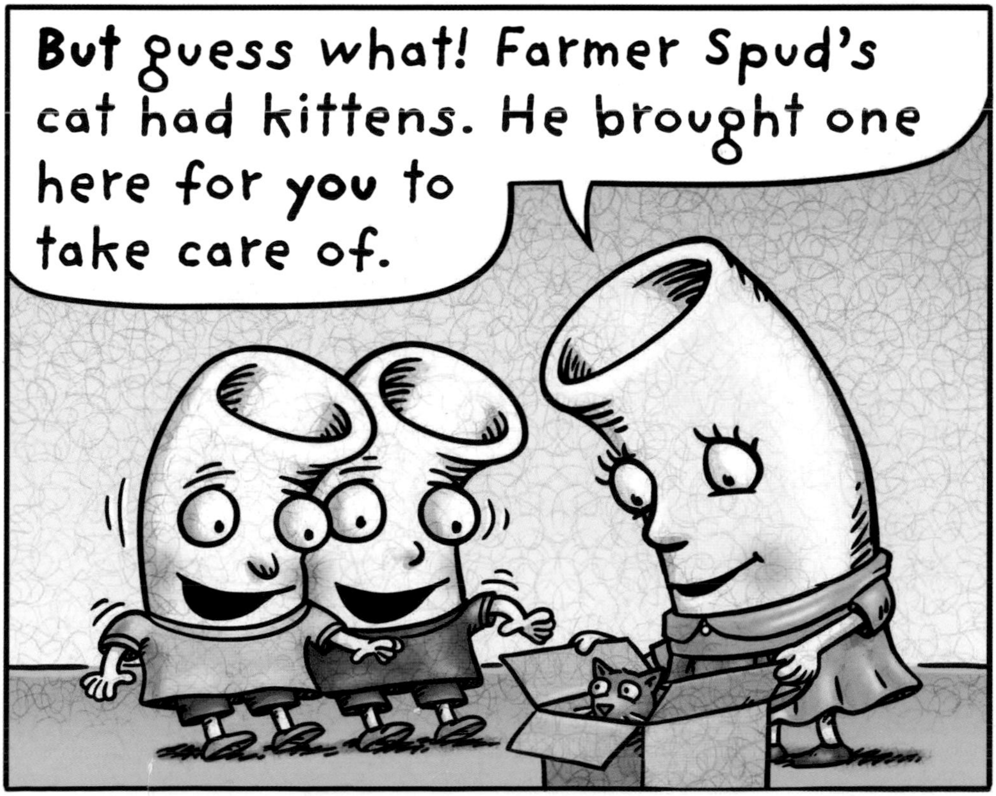
But guess what! Farmer Spud's cat had kittens. He brought one here for you to take care of.

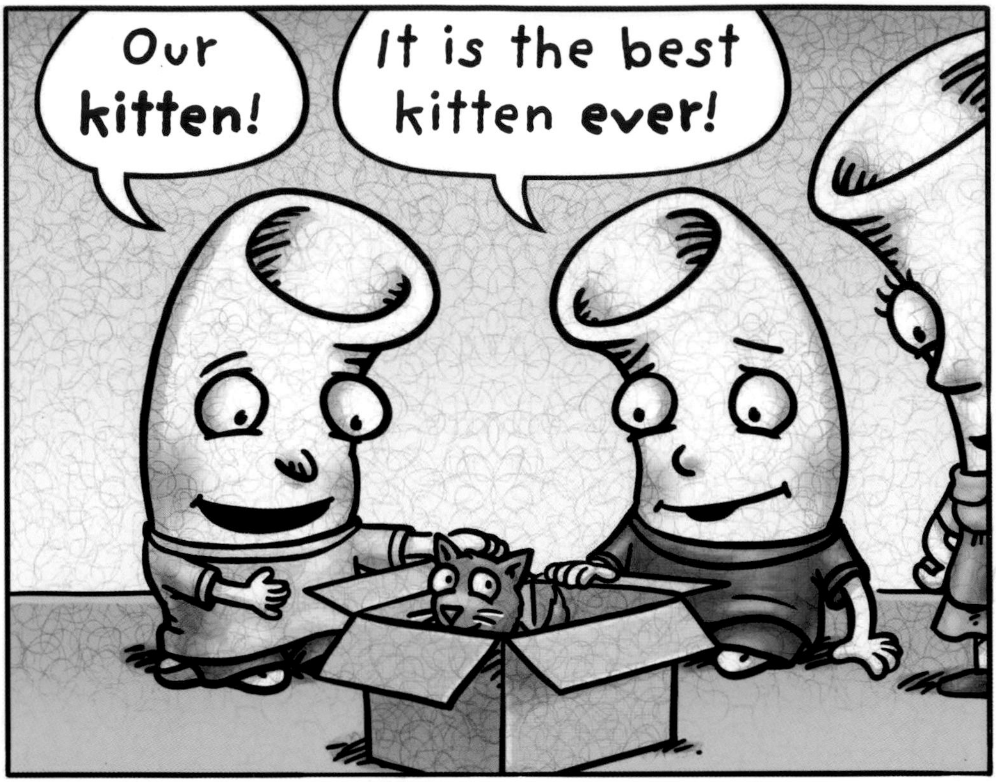
Our kitten!
It is the best kitten ever!

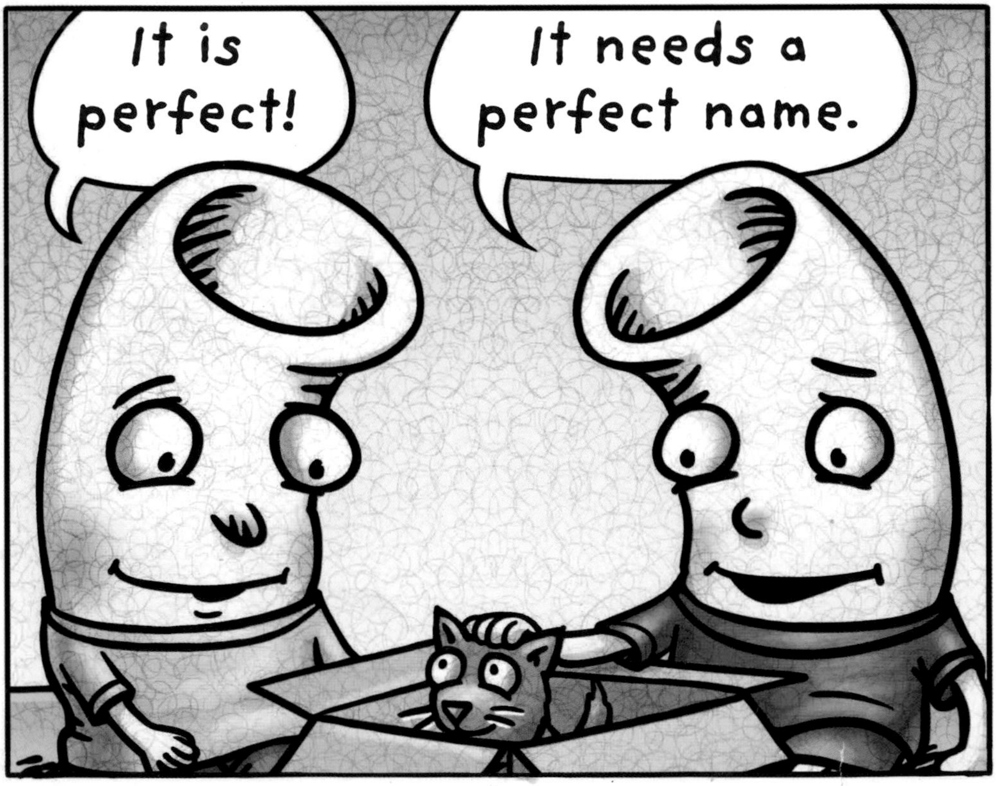
It is perfect!
It needs a perfect name.

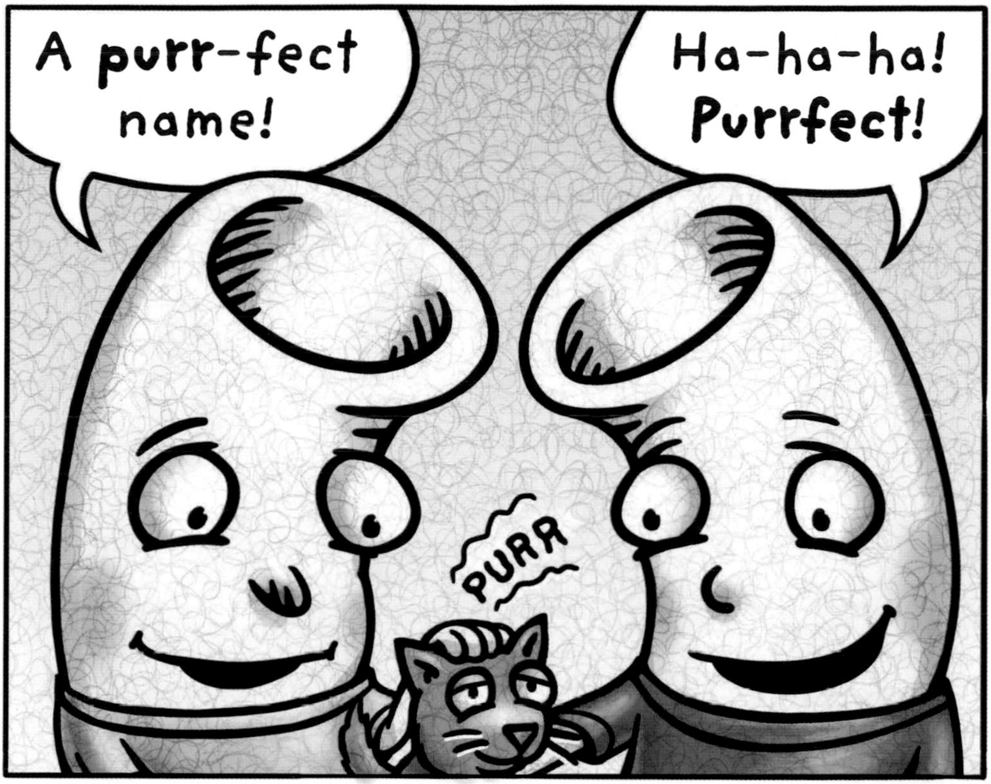
A purr-fect name!
Ha-ha-ha! Purrfect!
PURR

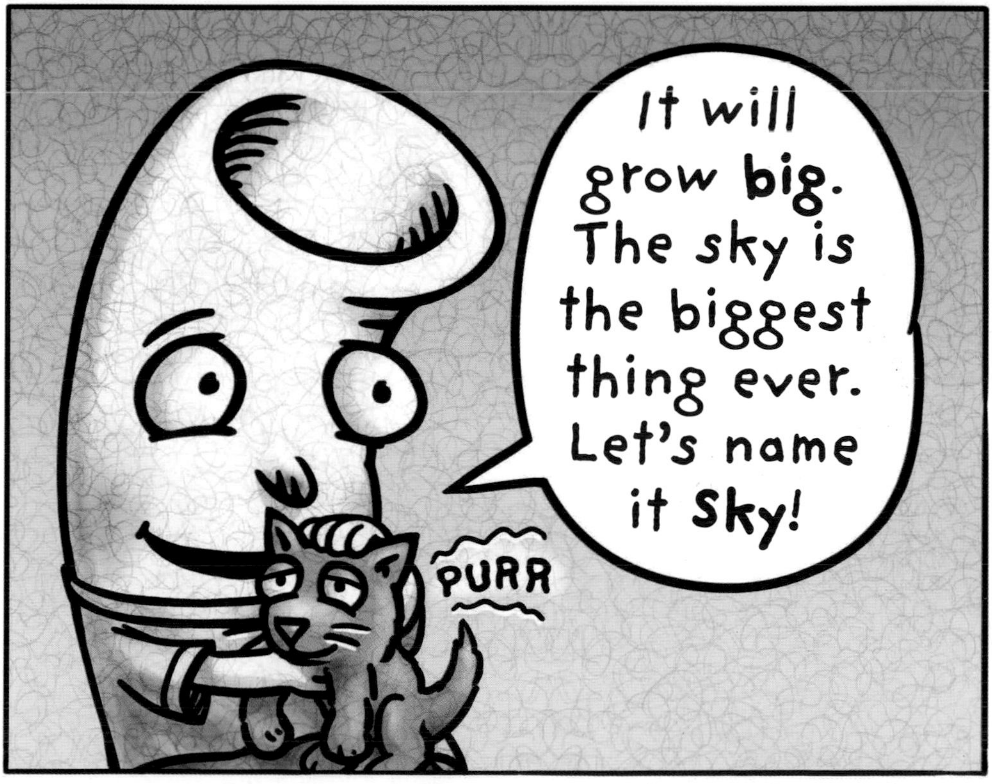
It will grow big. The sky is the biggest thing ever. Let's name it Sky!
PURR

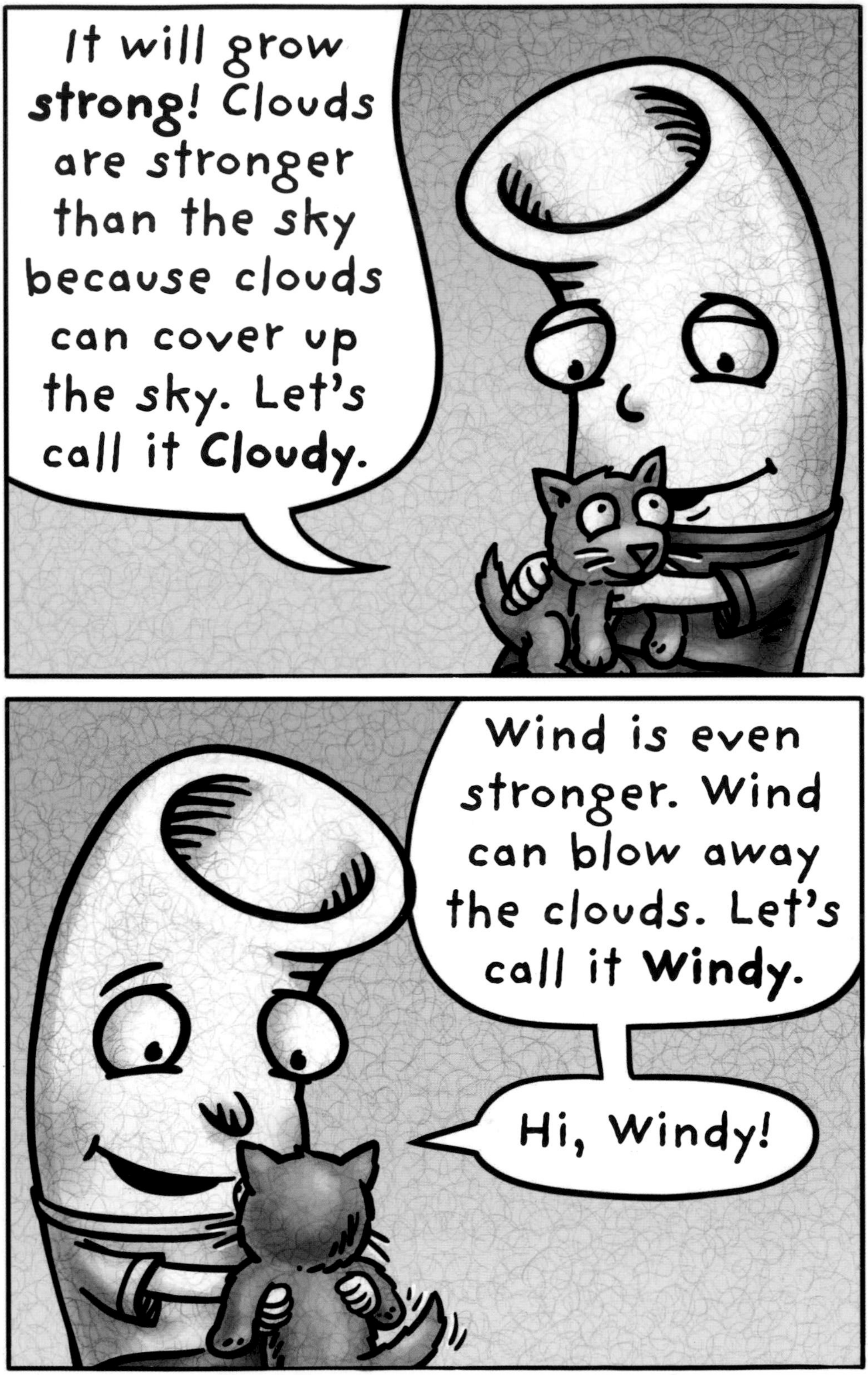
It will grow strong! Clouds are stronger than the sky because clouds can cover up the sky. Let's call it Cloudy.
Wind is even stronger. Wind can blow away the clouds. Let's call it Windy.
Hi, Windy!

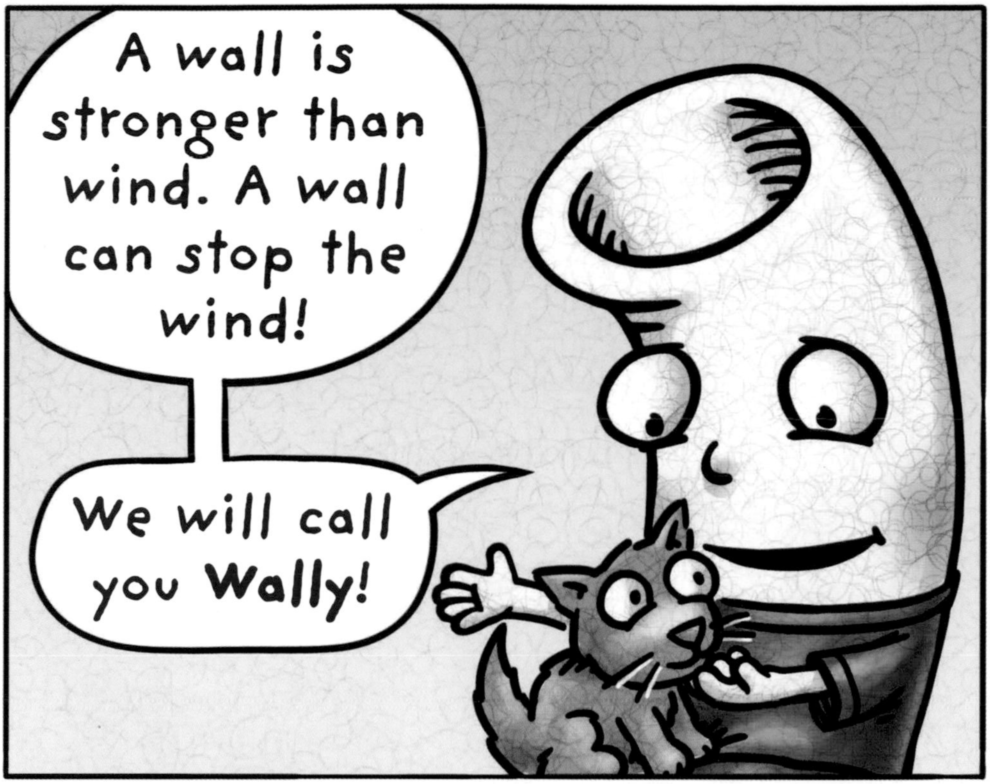
A wall is stronger than wind. A wall can stop the wind!
We will call you **Wally**!

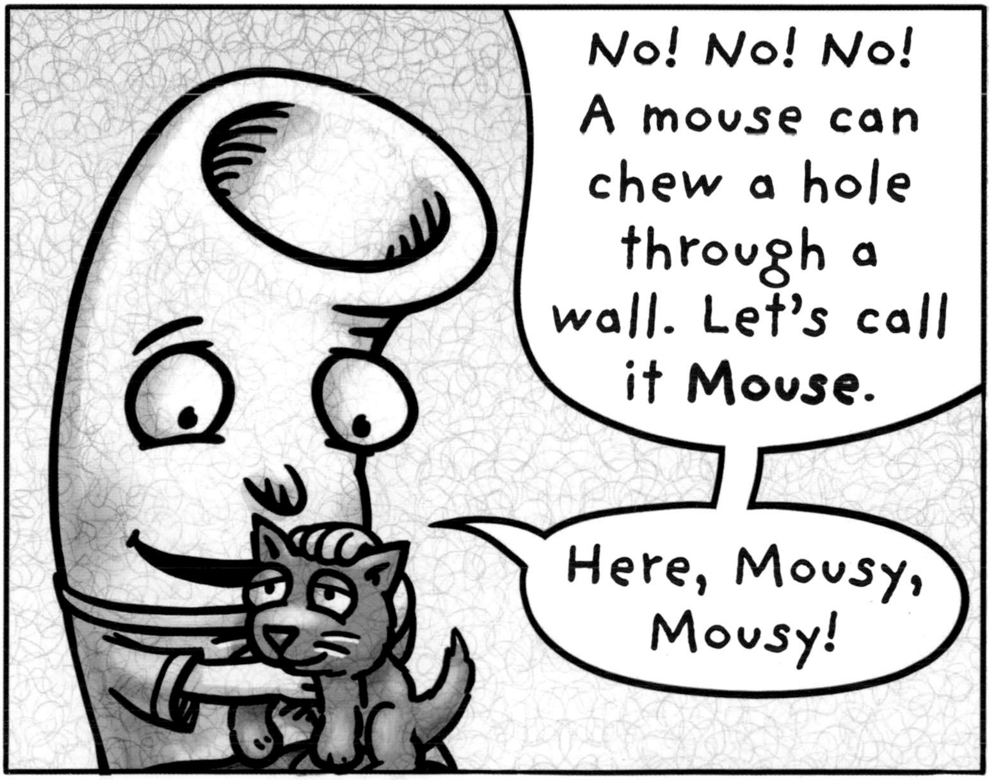
No! No! No! A mouse can chew a hole through a wall. Let's call it **Mouse**.
Here, Mousy, Mousy!

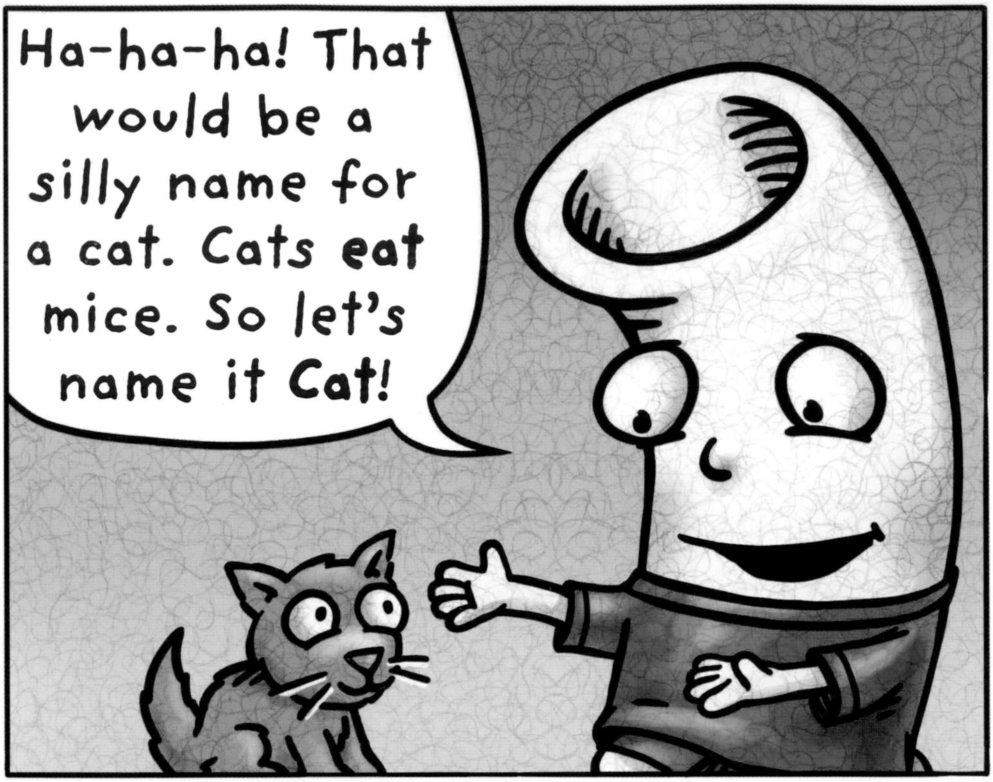
Ha-ha-ha! That would be a silly name for a cat. Cats eat mice. So let's name it Cat!
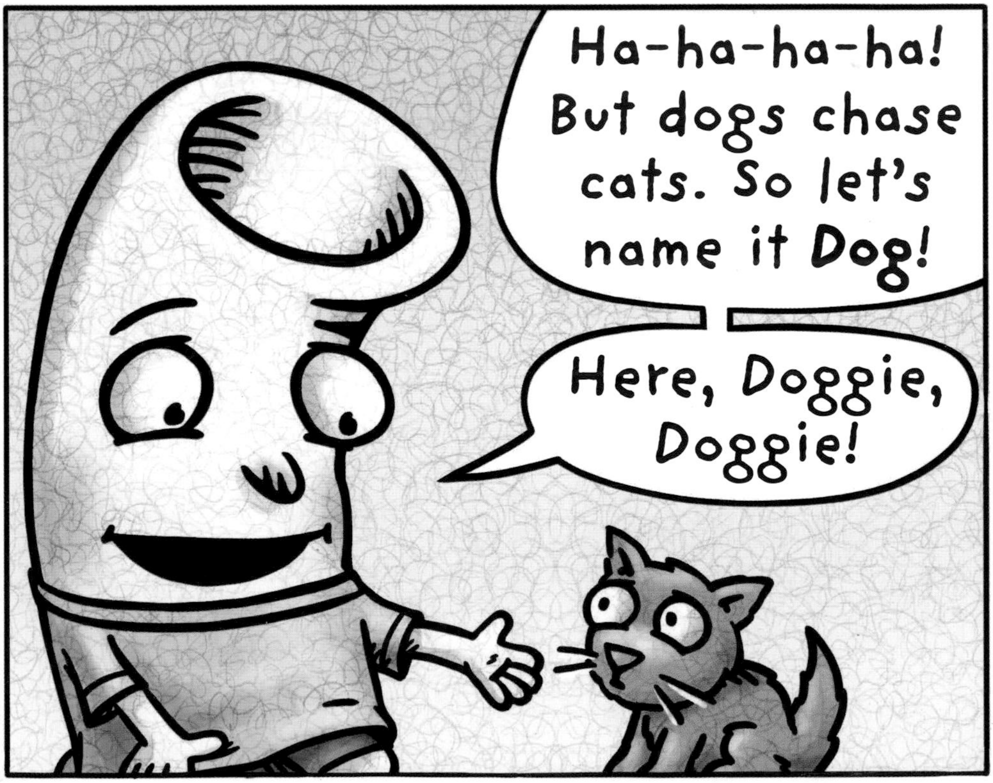
Ha-ha-ha-ha! But dogs chase cats. So let's name it Dog!
Here, Doggie, Doggie, Doggie!

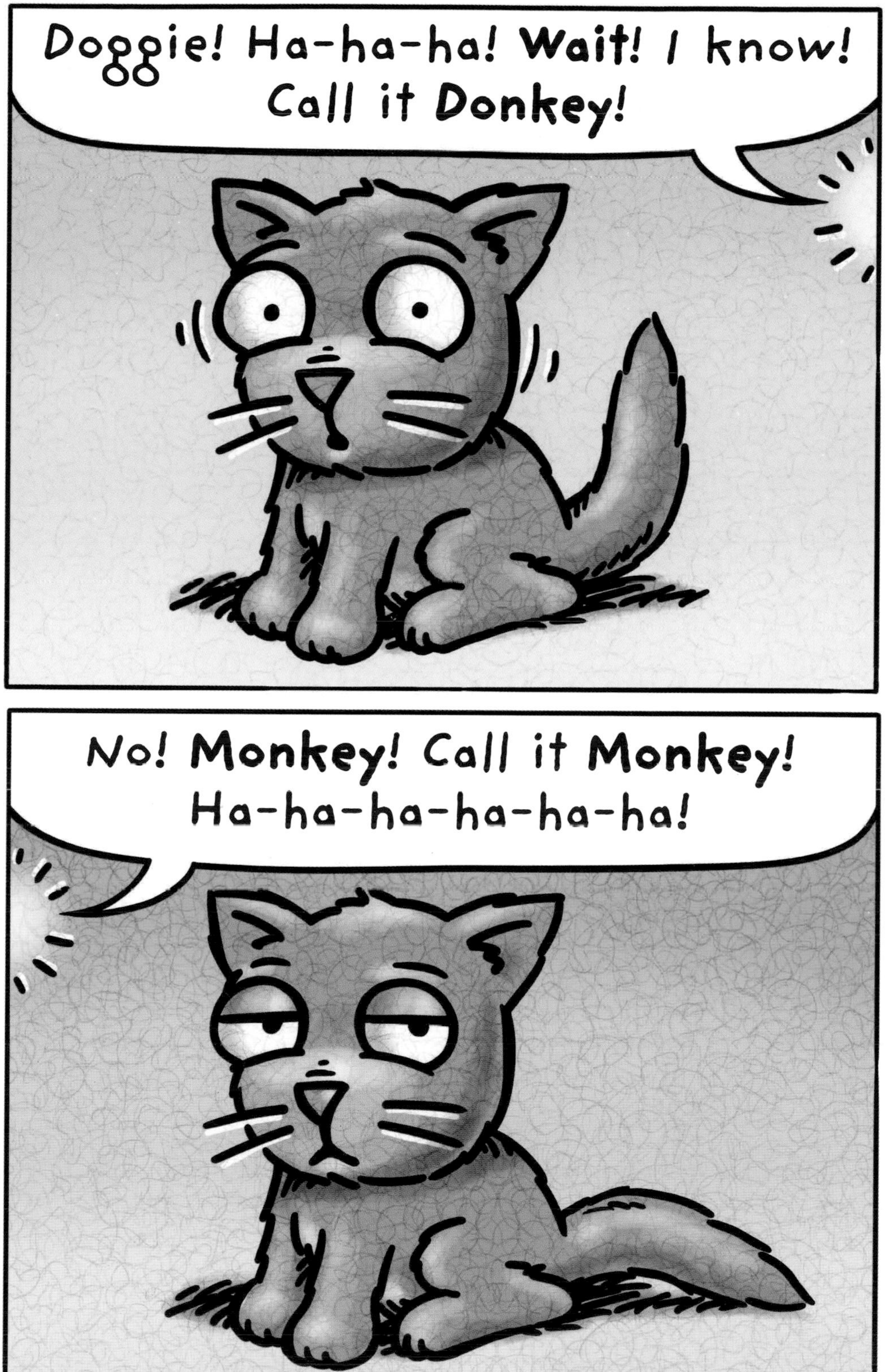
Doggie! Ha-ha-ha! Wait! I know! Call it Donkey!
No! Monkey! Call it Monkey! Ha-ha-ha-ha-ha-ha!

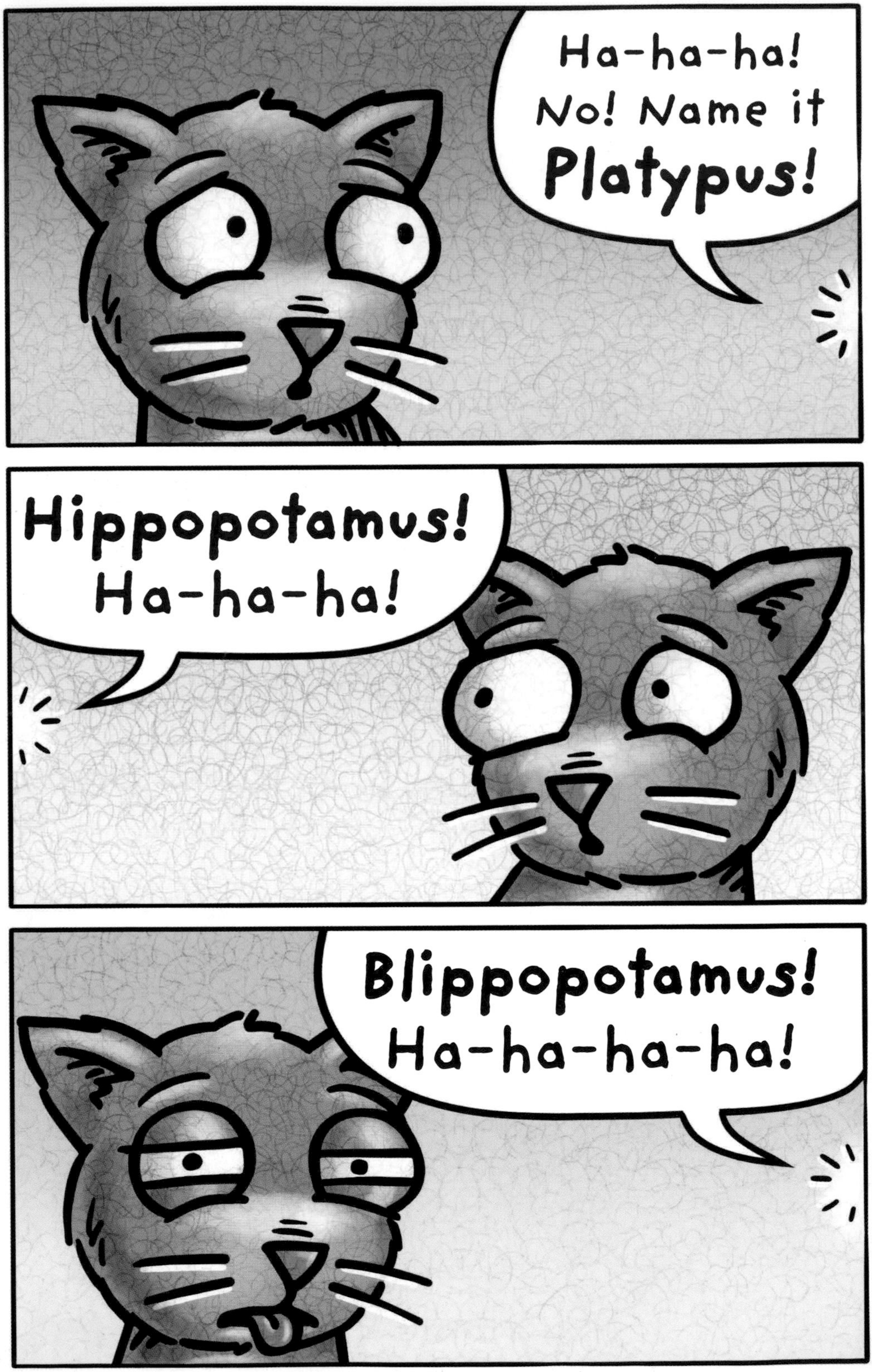
Ha-ha-ha! No! Name it Platypus!
Hippopotamus! Ha-ha-ha!
Blippopotamus! Ha-ha-ha-ha!

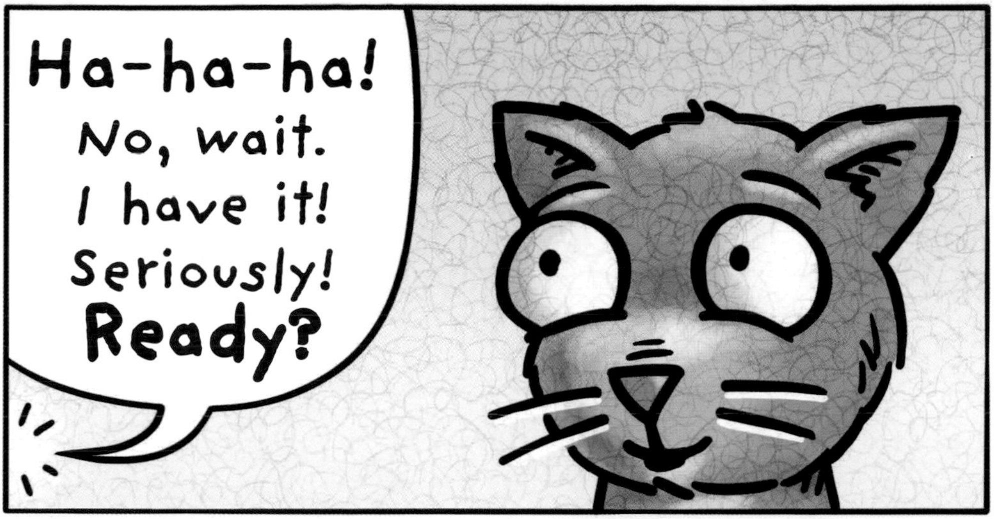
Ha-ha-ha!
No, wait.
I have it!
Seriously!
Ready?

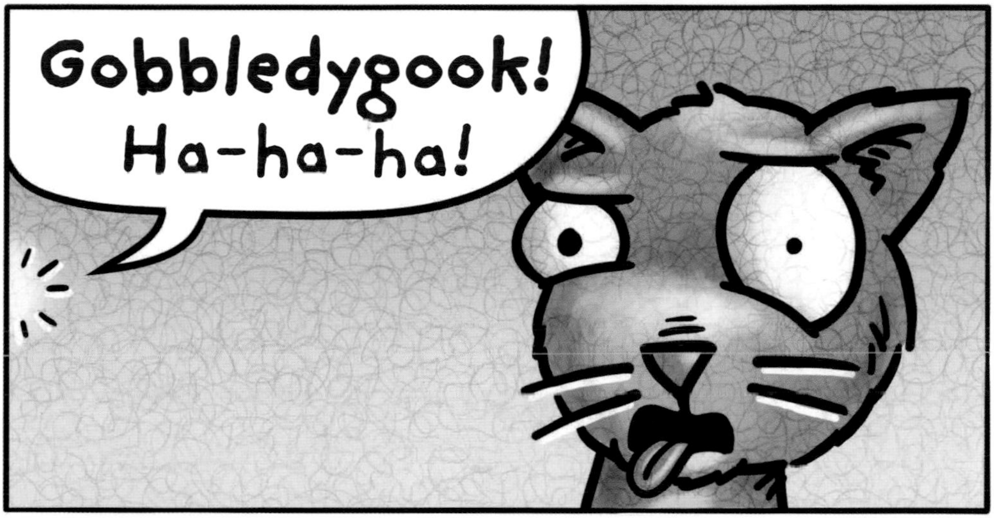
Gobbledygook!
Ha-ha-ha!

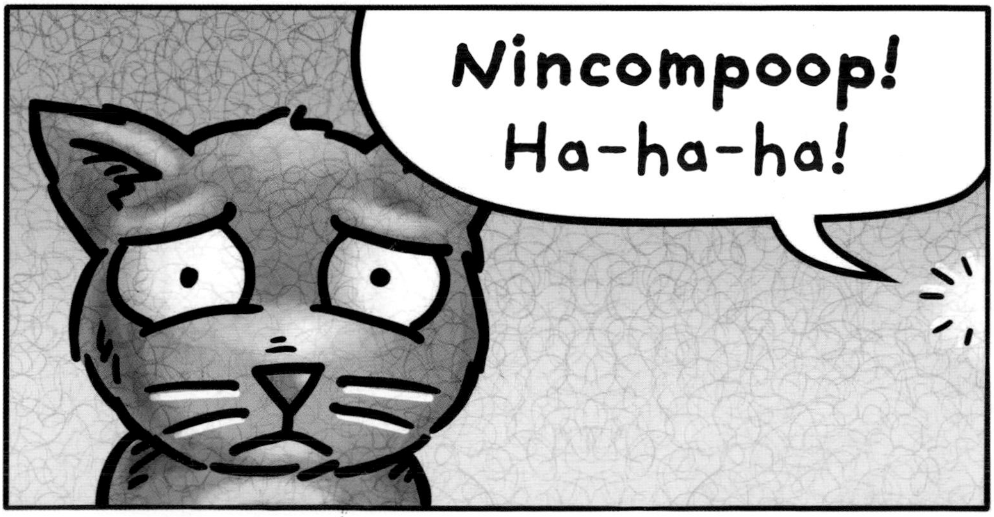
Nincompoop!
Ha-ha-ha!

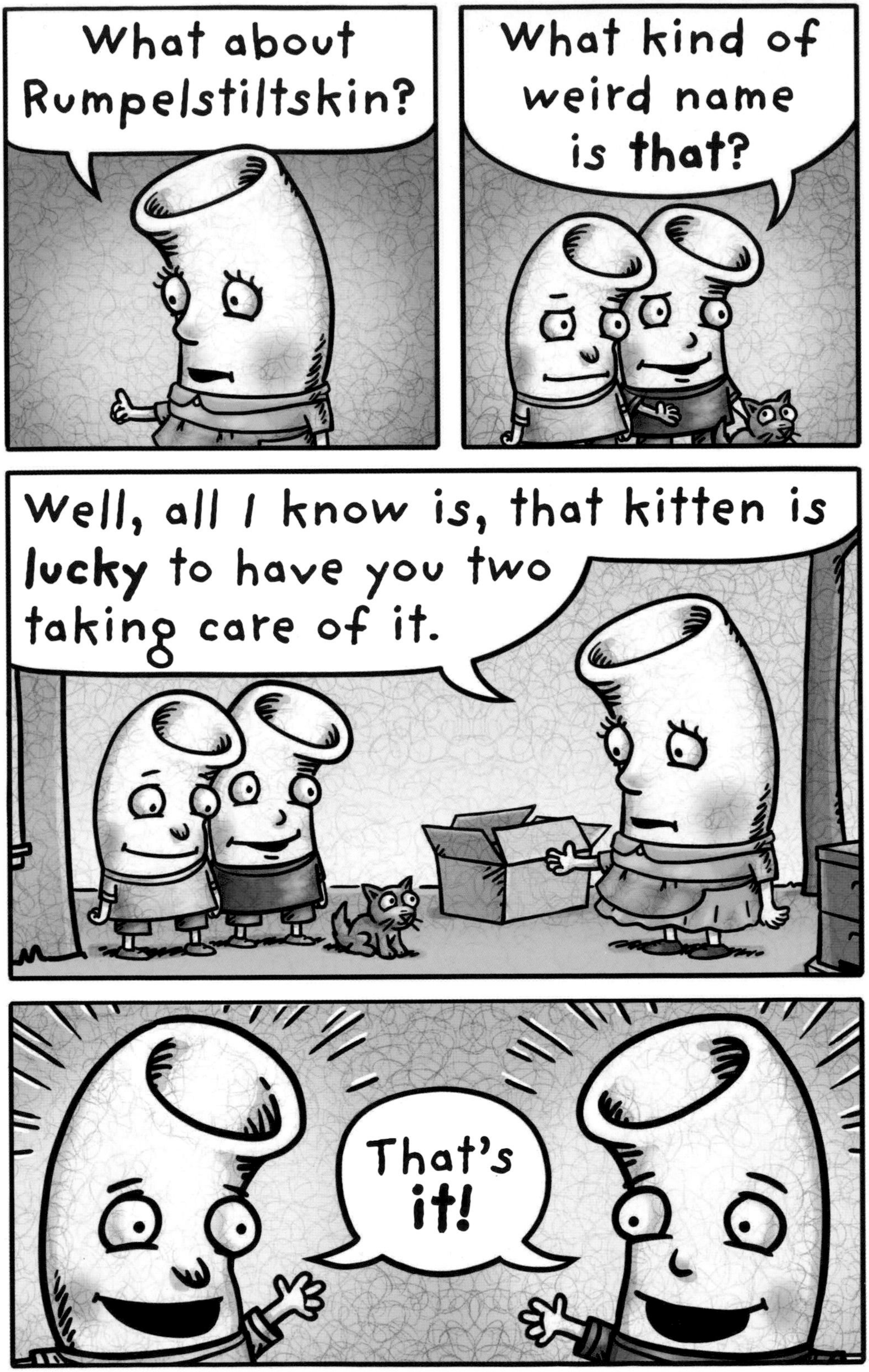

What about Rumpelstiltskin?
What kind of weird name is **that**?
Well, all I know is, that kitten is **lucky** to have you two taking care of it.
That's **it!**

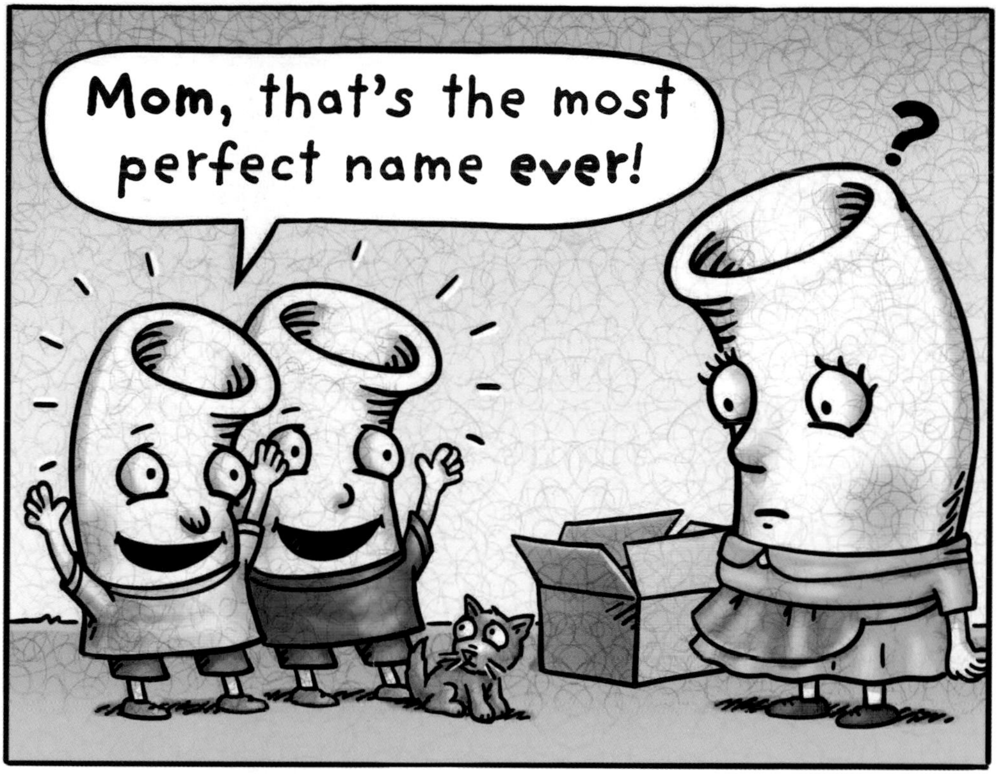
Mom, that's the most perfect name ever!
?

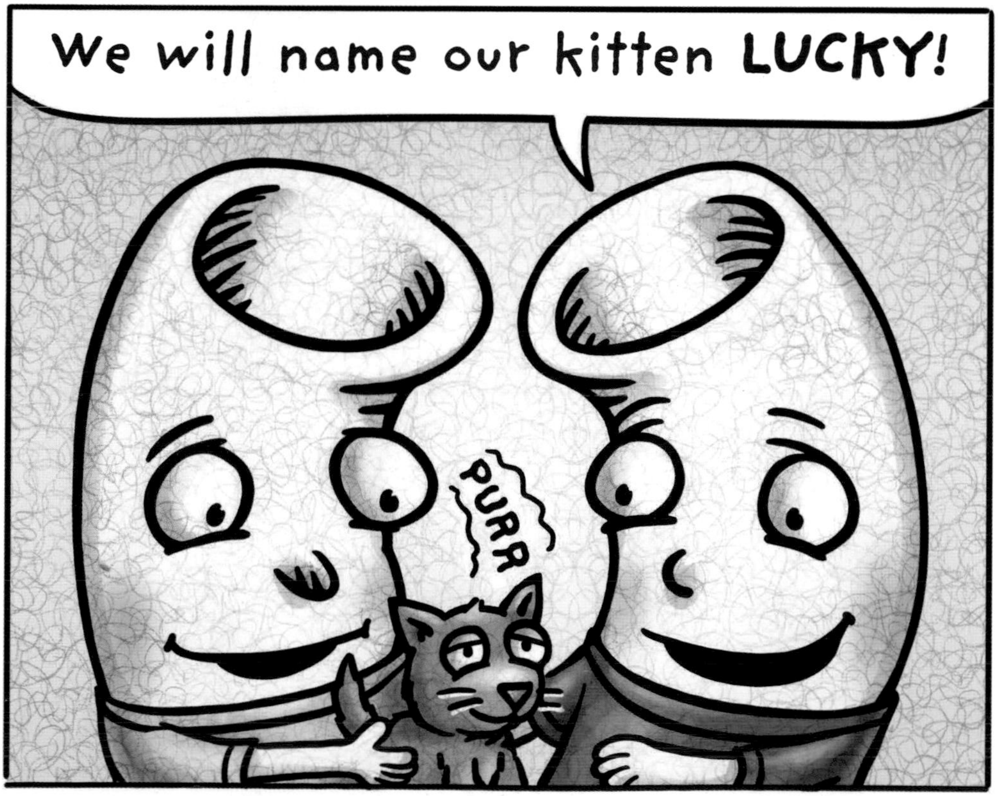
We will name our kitten LUCKY!
PURR

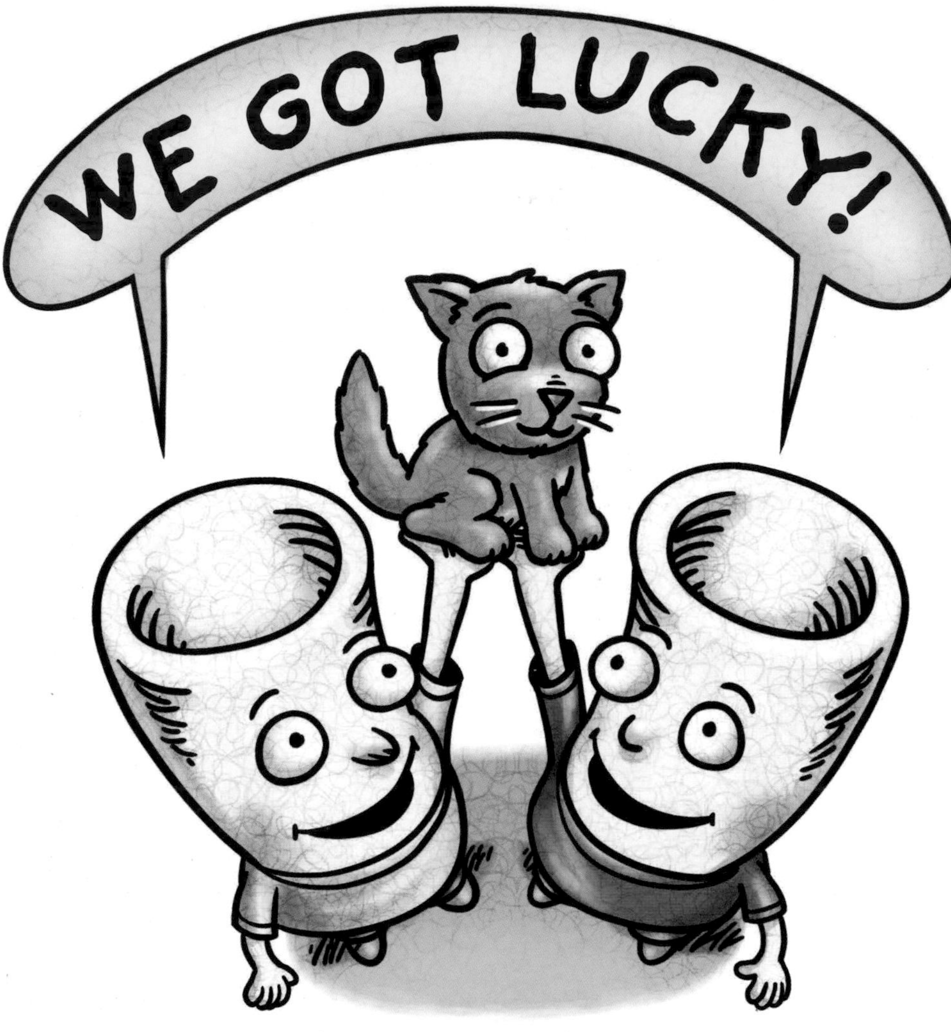
WE GOT LUCKY!

Authors' Notes
Story Sources for Noodleheads Lucky Day

Old tales about fools, who were also called "noodles" or "noodleheads," are the inspiration for Mac and Mac's adventures in our Noodleheads series. In 1888, W. A. Clouston wrote a scholarly book called *The Book of Noodles* in which he described numerous stories that had been told for hundreds of years, with quite a few dating back over two millennia. People around the world tell similar stories about their particular fools, such as Giufà in Italy, Nasreddin Hodja in Turkey, Juan Bobo in Puerto Rico, and Jack in England. These world tales remind us of our shared humanity; we have all done or said something foolish, and the stories give us a chance to laugh at ourselves.

"Fool's luck" and "Fortune favors fools" are common expressions. When presented with a dilemma, some folks consider all options, carefully calculate, and use their best judgment to make what seems to be the smartest decision. That behavior usually rewards them with a good outcome. However, sometimes everything goes wrong. Perhaps their calculations were incorrect—or it might just have been bad luck. On the other hand, some folks procrastinate, avoid making a decision, and even deny that there is a problem. This behavior usually has serious consequences. When, as sometimes happens, everything still turns out fine, we call it "fool's luck."

Fool's luck plays a prominent role in folktales. For example, Jack, the famous fool of English folktales, trades the family's most valuable possession, their cow, for a few "magic" beans—but the beans end up truly being magical and bring him great wealth. In spite of their foolishness, things usually turn out fine in the end for noodleheads, perhaps because they are generally kind and well meaning. Children find comfort in the fact that a foolish mistake usually doesn't mean the end of the world. Even if Mac and Mac don't learn from their mistakes, children who read about their adventures do. Noodlehead stories also help us understand humor, logical thinking, and the importance of distinguishing between what's true and what's a lie. Children quickly see that they should not always believe what they hear, especially when the source is a bully like Meatball.

The motifs to which we refer in the information that follows are from *The Storyteller's Sourcebook: A Subject, Title, and Motif Index to Folklore Collections for Children* by Margaret Read MacDonald, first edition (Detroit: Gale, 1982), and second edition by Margaret Read MacDonald and Brian W. Sturm (Detroit: Gale, 2001). Tale types are from *A Guide to Folktales in the English Language* by D. L. Ashliman (NY: Greenwood, 1987).

Introduction

The motif that inspired this incident is J2571, *Thank fortune it wasn't a melon.* Mitch and Martha referred to several versions about Nasreddin Hodja, the wise fool of Turkey, for their retelling, "Watermelons and Walnuts," which can be found in *Through the Grapevine: World Tales Kids Can Read and Tell* (Atlanta: August House, 2001).

Chapter 1: Looking for Trouble

This story was inspired by trickster tales about characters who are fooled by someone because they are not familiar with words such as "trouble" or "misery." Similar motifs are K1055.2, *Dupe gets into grass to meet "Trouble,"* and J1805.2, *Monkey thinks syrup is called "Misery."* In a version found in Diane Wolkstein's *The Magic Orange Tree and Other Haitian Folktales,* the monkey asks for more misery and is given a sack full of dogs. Bees and hornets are often used for similar deceptions. We brainstormed ways that Meatball's trick could turn out to be lucky for Mac and Mac, and came up with their mom needing bees because she had just built hives.

Chapter 2: How to Hatch a Cat

Inspiration for this chapter came from tale type 1319, *Fool thinks pumpkin is a horse's egg.* The motifs are J1772.1, *Pumpkin thought to be an ass's egg,* and J1881.2, *Animal sent to go by itself.* Mitch and Martha's retelling, "The Donkey Egg," can be found in *Noodlehead Stories: World Tales Kids Can Read and Tell* (Atlanta: August House, 2000). It was adapted from an Algerian version in Clouston's *Book of Noodles.* Similar stories are found in China, India, France, Switzerland, the United States, and Russia.

Chapter 3: The Perfect Name

The idea for this chapter came from a Vietnamese tale about finding the perfect name for a cat. A version can be found in *The Toad Is the Emperor's Uncle: Animal Folktales from Viet-Nam* by Vo-Dinh (Garden City, NY: Doubleday, 1970), pp. 123–128. The motif is L392.0.4, *Name of strongest creature sought for cat.* The progression from "Sky" to "Cat" and the arguments for each name are similar to Mac and Mac's. It seemed fitting that they would get the giggles after their funny "Mouse" and "Cat" suggestions. Their argument then devolves into silliness until their mom suggests "Rumpelstiltskin," a reference to the well-known German folktale from the Brothers Grimm.